This Is Always

Also by Ronald E. Kimmons

An Infinity of Interpretations
*A Bit of Social Commentary on and a Philosophical
Examination of Life in These Times*

After the Laughter
A Novel

This Is Always
A Novel

Ronald E. Kimmons

THIS IS ALWAYS
A NOVEL

iUniverse books may be ordered through booksellers or by contacting:

iUniverse
1663 Liberty Drive
Bloomington, IN 47403
www.iuniverse.com
844-349-9409

ISBN: 978-1-6632-2969-4 (sc)
ISBN: 978-1-6632-2970-0 (hc)
ISBN: 978-1-6632-2968-7 (e)

Library of Congress Control Number: 2021920172

Print information available on the last page.

iUniverse rev. date: 09/27/2021

Contents

About the Author

Ronald E. Kimmons is a retired educator who spent almost four decades in the field of education in various positions (teacher, counselor, administrator, college instructor). He received his doctor of philosophy degree in 2002 from the University of Chicago.

The author has written two books prior to this one. His first book, *An Infinity of Interpretations*, is a nonfiction book. That book is a bit of social commentary and a philosophical examination of life in these times. His second book, *After the Laughter*, is a fiction book about a young man's existential quest to find meaning for his life. In both of his prior books, the author has tried to provide readers with interesting and meaningful materials that cross several genres but are still ultimately deeply rooted in matters related to the human condition.

He was born in Chicago. He now lives in Chicago.

Dedication

To

Rosa Davis
My maternal grandmother

Vicki and Cydney
My daughters and the true loves of my life

Erin. Arthur (III), and Arthur (IV)
My grandchildren and great-grandson, the other true loves of my life

Arthur, Jr.
Their father

My siblings and parents: Bertram, Donald, Wally Rose, Wayne, Frank, Mildred, Herbert, Exzene, Talmadge, Eugene, Jr., Eugene, and Alberta

Always there to support me in whatever I was doing—what a great family

Epigraph

"To be a Negro in this country and to be relatively conscious is to be in a rage almost all the time."

James Baldwin

"If black racial identity speaks to all the things done to people of recent African ancestry, black cultural identity was created in response to them. The division is not neat; the two are linked, and it is incredibly hard to be a full participant in the world of cultural identity without experiencing the trauma of racial identity."

TaHesi Coates

Both of the quotations above reflect a truth about the African-American experience in America, but it is only a partial truth. The whole truth would also have to talk about the joy often seen in the life of African Americans and the beauty and grace often exhibited by African Americans in daily life and on special occasions.

This book is mostly about the joy, beauty, and grace of African Americans told from the viewpoint of a young, Black man who grew up on the South Side of Chicago. This book also chronicles how the joy, beauty, and grace of African Americans helped African Americans survive in America and give the world pieces of a transcendent culture now embraced and enjoyed around the world.

Prologue

Life as lived by Blacks in particular and other minorities, in general, is different from the life that is lived by folks who are in the majority—and this is the case everywhere in the world. There is a gravitas or heaviness like none other that pervades the existence of any minority—now and any time in the past. The question is this: Does the minority live in the gravitas or on it? That is more than a philosophical question, and the answer determines the way of life for a people.

Most of what we hear, read, and think about life in America for African Americans tends to take the position that they have lived in the gravitas. Without a doubt, there is some truth to that. But it is only a partial truth. If you believe and or see only the partial truth of a life lived in the gravitas, you will miss what Stanley Crouch says is a "nuanced vision of the grandeur of the human heart."

This story offers the reader a journey into the life of a people told from the viewpoint of a young man who both lived in (within the limits of) and on (above) the gravitas and who was a witness to the nuanced vision of the grandeur of the human heart and the grandeur of the people who produced that vision. As such, this story is both nonfiction and fiction—probably closer to historical fiction if you do not like propositions with conjunctives or words such as "and" or "or."

Although the central force for this story came into existence many millennia ago, the year 1939 is a pivotal point in this story. That is the year the protagonist of our story was born and the same year that the mother of all wars started. The first day of the first month of 1939 was his birthday, and the first day of the ninth month of 1939 was the start of the war that was the deadliest in all of history—one estimate puts the count of the dead as high as 85 million.

While Europeans and their various allies, including America, warred mightily against one another for the first half of the 20th Century, his family and millions like them migrated out of the bellicose and economically declining South to the West, Northeast, and Midwest areas of the United States to avoid warring against their oppressors, although some of that happened, too.

In this tale, the year 1939 is also important because it is the year that Charlie Parker came to the South Side of Chicago and played for several weeks at the Club Delisa over on 55th and State. Charlie Parker was significant to this young man not only because of the way he played the alto saxophone but also because he made manifest an archetype that represented the people who were able to produce that nuanced vision of the grandeur of the heart.

Others could have been archetypes for the people who produced a nuanced vision of the grandeur of the human heart, but Parker was a progenitor or originator of musicians you can now see around the globe in places such as Paris, London, Rome, Venice, Madrid, Berlin, Moscow, Barcelona, Bombay, Beijing, Sydney, Johannesburg, and other major cities around the world.

But the nuanced vision of the grandeur of the human heart had its beginnings centuries before the young man was born and before the deadliest war in history was started and before Charlie Parker came to Chicago to play at the Club Delisa. It all began many millennia ago in Africa where the drums of the Yoruba people mimicked the human heartbeat and set in motion the quintessence of all creativity: To give expression to what one can only feel—to imagine the invisible and to make that known or knowable in one form or another. The rhythm of the drums creates the framework for most of the creativity that comes to us in so many forms in the African American community and other communities throughout the world. But that framework had both preceded and accompanied him at birth on a cold winter morning in 1939.

Chapter One
Beauty and Grace

His mother later told Gregory that in anticipation of his arrival, the world had rejoiced in and celebrated his arrival a few hours before he made his entrance into the world and this life. That was a story Gregory liked having told to him. It always made him feel special. And because he felt special, he felt the people in his life and world were special.

So instead of seeing his life and the people who surrounded him only through the prisms of racism, oppression, and violence; Gregory mostly saw beauty and grace— both expressions of a nuanced vision of the grandeur of the human heart. He saw beauty in the people, art, music, theater, literature, and general aesthetics of the world he lived in. He was a witness to grace in the athleticism, dance, dress, and movements of ordinary people he saw every day and extraordinary people he saw on special occasions.

Most of Gregory's early life was spent with him ensconced in a fairly large and closely-knit family that lived on the South Side of Chicago, not far from the Illinois Institute of Technology (made famous by Mies van der Rohe) and Comiskey Park (home of the Chicago White Sox).

These institutions would provide images and ideas and thoughts for Gregory's ever-burgeoning view of the world. But his most impressionable images and ideas and thoughts came from the nearby neighborhood, the house he lived in, and the people who inhabited that house.

One of the people who inhabited that house was also one of the ordinary people whose movements Gregory loved to watch. That person was his maternal grandmother. He could remember images of his grandmother in his mind and in pictures in which she was alone or with her siblings. His grandmother's sister (who looked mixed with American Indian blood of some kind) and his grandmother's brother (who looked as if he could have been straight out of Africa) sat stoically and proud as the camera captured and stored images which would later be viewed in various formats and venues for the next century.

It was as a young boy viewing the pictures of his grandmother and her siblings that he first became conscious of the beauty and grace of the world he had been brought into.

He was always grateful to his grandmother for all of the things she taught him and that would enhance his life as he grew older. In addition to teaching him how to cook and sew, his grandmother also taught him how to clean a house so that it was not only cleaned but also shined.

At first, he did not see the difference between cleaned and shined, but his grandmother had a way of showing him how to tilt his head a little to see the shine she wanted in anything he had to clean. After a point, he took that perspective on most of what he did in life. He equated cleaned with doing a job. He equated shined with doing a job well or as near to perfection as you could.

He also learned from his grandmother how to move his body in space—of any kind—quietly and almost in slow motion—some would say phlegmatically. He loved to watch her cooking or tending a small garden next to the apartment building in which they lived or just sitting and eating and talking with the family at dinner time.

Here was one of his first conscious and earthly embodiments of beauty and grace.

When his grandmother died, he remembered being sad and hurt, but he remembered vividly that he did not cry at her funeral. That struck him as being odd because he had always associated grief with tears, and he deeply felt the grief that accompanied his grandmother's death.

Whenever he thought about his grandmother's passing and his failure or inability to cry in relationship to that event, he had alternative beliefs about why he did not cry. One belief had to do with the fact that he had constantly watched his grandmother in the days shortly before her death on the let-out sofa in the living room that was her bed; he did not see how it was possible that she could or would die.

She never complained about anything and never appeared to be in pain of any kind. So, on the evening she passed and was pronounced dead by the family physician and taken to the funeral home, he had assumed she was just being taken to the hospital where they would discover she was still alive. Her returning home was simply a matter of time.

When that did not happen, his next belief was that his grandmother had decided to leave the family and go to heaven to get some rest from all of the burdens she had to bear in relationship to all of the children in the family and the demands they made on her.

He believed she would return from heaven after she had laid down some of her burdens. So, death was not only an inevitable event but also an existential choice which could override that inevitable event. That made so much sense to him, it was years before he would abandon that belief in favor of ones that were more based on facts and reality.

At an early age, he had tried to get his mother to talk about how she and his father had met and made the decision to come to Chicago. He never got far with that part of the story, but his mother would offer up tidbits about how various members of the family had gone from different parts of the South to a part of Chicago variously described as The Black Belt, The Stroll, Bronzeville, The South Side, and other (in some cases, not so nice and racist) terms.

Over the years, he was able to piece together a coherent if not a complete picture of his family's story related to The Great Migration. Ultimately, he realized it was a great migration within the Great Migration for his family (and many other families).

The story as Gregory remembered it was that his family was among the hundreds of thousands who left various states of the South during this time; but those who came to Chicago mostly came from Arkansas, Mississippi, Georgia, Alabama, and Louisiana. Like his family, many migrants from the South made a stop in Memphis, Tennessee, which is where his mother and father had met and married and where his oldest brother had been born.

His mother was out of Mississippi, and his father was out of Little Rock, Arkansas. He would find out later that Little Rock was not his father's birthplace, despite what his father had told the family for many years and what was on his father's death certificate. His father had been born in Helena, Arkansas, a small town on the Mississippi River not too far from Memphis and half the distance from Little Rock to Memphis.

His mother had been born in another town on the Mississippi River, Vicksburg, whose notoriety mainly stemmed from its defeat during the Civil War and the wholesale lynching of Blacks by members of the Ku Klux Klan. Shortly after his mother was born, in 1904, her family had opted to move to a safer place farther east and north: Greenville, Mississippi. It was not a good move, however.

Although Greenville had been rebuilt after the Civil War on the highest point between Vicksburg and Memphis, the Great Mississippi Flood of 1927 flooded most of the area below Memphis and forced more than a half-million people to relocate. That flood is not much talked about in books and media detailing the Great Migration. Still, it is a major accelerant for the movement of Blacks from the South in general and the deltas of Mississippi and Arkansas in particular.

His mother had been brought into the world as the result of an ongoing liaison between a pretty Black woman (his grandmother) and a man from a small band of Choctaw Indians who remained in Greenville after the Choctaw negotiated a treaty which moved that Indian nation to lands in the Oklahoma Territory. The liaison ended when the man, in response to family pressure, decided to move to Oklahoma in 1907 to join his family in the newly established state of Oklahoma. His grandmother decided to stay in Greenville with her only child (his mother) and subsequently married a Black man who had been brought to the plantation where she labored as a sharecropper from a nearby plantation farther north.

His grandparents on his mother's side spent the next two decades sharecropping and raising four children they were responsible for. It was not a great life, but they managed to eke out a living and find some happiness within the community down there in the Mississippi Delta.

By the time the Great Mississippi Flood of 1927 occurred, his family had already talked about moving north to take advantage of the economic and political freedoms being broadcasted by the *Chicago Defender* and individuals who occasionally came home to visit from the north sporting fine clothes and driving fancy cars, some of which may have been borrowed or rented for the trip home.

Before the Great Mississippi Flood of 1927 happened, there had been warnings and signs there would be trouble in cities and towns bordering the Mississippi river if the river ever overflowed its banks. The Army Corps of Engineers had even attempted to build levees to mitigate the damage that might occur if such an event ever happened. But as surely as the sun will rise, nature will do the unexpected; or in this case, the expected. In the spring of 1927, there were several breaks in the levees of the Mississippi River in Illinois and Mississippi that put more than 27,000 square miles of land underwater, 30 feet of water in some places.

In an area below Memphis and at the beginnings of the southern deltas of Mississippi and Arkansas, the flooding caused thousands of families, including his mother's family, to move from Greenville to points farther north and east of Mississippi and Arkansas. They wound up first in Memphis and then hopscotched to Cairo, St. Louis, Peoria,

Argo-Summit, and Chicago. And by the time he was born in 1939, ten of his siblings had already entered this world and begun their efforts to survive and make sense of this thing we call life.

Gregory had always wondered about his family's affinity for towns on the mighty Mississippi River, but he recognized in some ways that that might have just been part of mankind's affinity for water around the world. He thought it also could have been because there was a particular affinity his family had for water as a spiritual connection to each other and to ancestors. And his family's affinity for water could have also been a symbolic way of thinking about how all of life connected and flowed into the presence—referring to both current existence and a supernatural influence often felt to be nearby.

When he first saw the mighty Mississippi River as a young man visiting St. Louis, Missouri, he was impressed. When he later saw the Mississippi River as an adult visiting St. Louis, he was awestruck. During that second visit to the river, he had all sorts of thoughts about what he had read in American literature and what he was able to learn as a student and, later, teacher of geography and history.

In his mind, he could almost see Huck Finn and Jim on a raft floating down the river, and he saw Union troops dying in an effort to overpower Confederate soldiers at Vicksburg. What he thought about most, however, was the conflict which arose when thousands of African Americans were forced to work without compensation with the American Red Cross' relief efforts during the Great Mississippi River Flood of 1927.

African Americans were by far the largest ethnic/racial group negatively affected by the Great Mississippi River Flood of 1927, especially in some regions of the South where they were concentrated both as laborers and citizens; so, in some sense, it made sense that they would work even without compensation, but in the Greenville area they were evacuated to and stranded on the crest of the Greenville Levee and forced to work for days without food or clean water. That and other events strained further the relationship between Blacks and Whites in this area during this time, and his family and other families decided to make the relatively short trek from Greenville to Memphis and other parts unknown.

Family lore had it that his father had walked part of the way from Helena to Memphis; and by the time he reached the outskirts of Memphis, he had to flip his feet up in the air a bit to make sure the soles of his shoes, which had torn loose from the shoe tops, hit the ground first instead of his bare feet.

There were also stories about how his father wandered around south Memphis (where most Blacks lived at the time) looking for food and shelter to hold him until he found a job.

His father was lucky because shortly after he arrived in Memphis, he found a cousin who helped him get a job at a large laundry company. That is where his father first saw his mother and made the decision that he was going to have her for his wife.

His mother's oft-repeated version of that first meeting with his father was that when he introduced himself to her, she told him she was not interested in dating "no high-yellow man" and told him to just keep stepping!

His grandmother, who also worked at the laundry in Memphis back then, added to the story by saying, "That's true. She did tell him that, but she also later confided in me that she did have some interest in pursuing a relationship with that 'high-yellow, good-looking man.'"

His mother always broadly smiled at that bit of correction of the facts of that matter. But it was always a smile seemingly laden with a bit of sadness and remorse. And he always carried some of that sadness and remorse for a while after he witnessed his mother in that state of mind and being, primarily because he felt his mother was always thinking about his father when she first met him and what he would eventually become.

His father did persuade his mother to marry him, and they had a son not long after that union was consummated. Out of fifteen children, that son was the only child born in Memphis. All of the others were born in Illinois, most of them in Chicago, although there was one other child who was stillborn in Memphis. When that first son was born, he was born with very dark skin and wavy hair; when he got older, everybody called him Dark Gable!

That son did not mind that epithet and wore it proudly for most of his life. He lived up to Gable's reputation as a ladies' man and had a habit of flashing a crooked grin that made everyone think of Gable. He was a charmer, for sure. But, in one way or another, so were all the males (ten in number) born to the family. Some years later, at the funeral of one of his nephews, one of the pretty and elegant ladies from the old neighborhood got up and talked about how as a young lady, she knew she was going to get her one of those fine and charming boys from his family.

When he was growing up, he had always thought of his older siblings, especially his brothers, as being much older than he was. It was only later in life that he realized that they were not that much older than him, especially the ones that he played in the streets with as a young boy and ran the streets with as a young man.

He never fully understood how or why he and his siblings were so close to one another, both in terms of age and affinity or love for one another. They had their differences as children and adults, but the tendency was more towards them enjoying each other's company and extending a helping hand when needed or required or just wanted. The thought of not speaking to or not wanting to be in the company of each other just did not happen. They were a close-knit family that seemed to always want to share.

One of his brothers closest to him in age had introduced him to the saxophone as the instrument of choice to play and listen to. Although in his house, he had always heard music playing from as far back as he could remember. There had been music playing from a variety of genres, but jazz was what was mostly heard: Gene Ammons, Sonny Stitt, Dizzy Gillespie, Charlie Parker, Louis Armstrong, Duke Ellington, Miles Davis, Thelonious Monk, Billie Holiday, Sarah Vaughn, Dinah Washington, Count Basie, John Coltrane, Frank Sinatra, Chet Baker, Stan Kenton, Dexter Gordon, McCoy Tyner, Ella Fitzgerald, Art Blakey, Horace Silver, Pharoah Sanders, and on and on. Of course, his all-time favorite was Charlie Parker, which he thought could have been influenced by his brother but more likely just because Parker was an outstanding musician.

He would later learn that when Charlie Parker first arrived in Chicago, he hung out at the Local 208 Musicians Union Hall on 39th and State, just two blocks east from where his family lived. The 208 was the Black side of the American Federation of Musicians unions in the Chicago area. It would be more than another quarter of a century for it to be integrated with the Local 10 Musicians Union, the White side of the American Federation of Musicians. The 208 had been the first black local musicians' union in America and had received its charter in 1902. It was fitting that Parker would hang out there, and even more fitting that he would find other musicians to play with to help him finally be able to play the sounds that he felt and had heard in his head and felt in his heart for years but could not give expression to.

By the time that Parker left Chicago and headed to New York for the second time, he already had hints of what he finally would be able to express in New York. Parker (now being referred to as "Bird") got help from a woman he met called Lydia, a jazz singer who worked the jazz clubs on the South Side of Chicago. One of the musicians who frequently went to the 208 to get work and pay dues had introduced Lydia to Parker.

Lydia was the kind of woman that didn't take shit from nobody! Every third word she spoke was a cuss word: motherfucker this and fucking that. Her mother was a well-known lady of the night in the small area of the South Side to which Blacks were confined and known locally as The Stroll.

As Gregory would learn over the years growing up on the South Side; initially, The

Stroll was geographically defined as an area on State Street (the dividing line between east and west in the street grid of Chicago) between 26th Street and 39th Street. Later the Stroll would encompass an area as far south as 47th Street and then 63rd Street. The expansion of the Stroll would become synonymous with conflicts between Blacks and Whites in Chicago for more than half a century, including a race riot that occurred in 1919 and left thirty-eight people dead, twenty-three blacks and fifteen whites.

Chapter Two
Everybody is Crazy

Another of those ordinary people whose movements he loved to watch was his father. His father was a dancer, socially, who often left the family on Friday or Saturday night to go alone to places not too far from where the family had settled on 38th and LaSalle, initially the farthest south and west boundaries of the narrow strip of land to which Blacks were then confined on Chicago's South Side after they left the trains at Grand Central Station near 12th Street and Michigan Avenue.

But those farthest boundaries were far enough. Just a few blocks east of the two-story flat where Gregory's family lived and on the other side of the tracks and viaduct were hotels, nightclubs, and other places where one could go to be and to be seen. Life, as lived in this area, was both gritty and grand at the same time.

No one in his family was ever sure of where his father went when he left home on Friday or Saturday night, but everyone was sure that he headed to some club on the Stroll to do what men did on the Stroll. And they never worried because at exactly midnight; he always hit the bottom step of the stairway that led to their two-bedroom apartment on the second floor of a building that was probably built around the end of the 19th century. When that happened, everyone in his family would relax, and sleep could earnestly begin for all who were home at that time. One evening, his father did not hit that first step at the time he was expected, and Gregory and his family began to worry.

His father was a very disciplined person, and punctuality was something he stressed even if you were having a good time. He and his siblings knew that something was wrong, and they decided to go looking for their father. It did not take long to find him. As he and his siblings turned the corner on 39th Street and headed for the train viaduct, they could see a thin figure standing in the dim lights under the viaduct. It was his father who stood there in just his shirt, underwear, and socks. Some fellows had robbed him, and they decided to take his tie, pants, jacket, and shoes, too. It would have been a funny scene, but he and his siblings thought he might have been hurt.

As they approached him, his father started to laugh, and they all joined in. He told them what had happened, including the fact that he was tipsy; but he said that the men had not harmed him much. They did hit him in the face once, but that was all. When they got home, he knew his mother was disgusted, but he watched as his mother lovingly tended to the bruise on his father's face and took him to bed.

The next day his father said that he wanted to sign himself into a state mental hospital. His mother cried and said he should try to wait it out and things would be better. His older brothers and sisters thought his father should at least have the chance to explore that idea. That was Sunday.

On Monday, his family checked around and found out that his father could sign himself into the hospital. His oldest brother and oldest sister agreed to take him. His father wanted to leave right away. That was the beginning of a series of stays in a mental hospital for his father over the next twenty years.

Those stays in the hospital by his father were painful and confusing to Gregory. He knew that his father both wanted and probably needed to be in the hospital, but he never had a sense of him getting better during those times when the family went to see him or during those periods when he was out of the hospital and home with the family.

What he did sense at times when he saw his father on the hospital grounds was a sense of contentment. The hospital was way out in the country, and it looked more like a college campus than it did the mental hospitals portrayed in movies and described in some books.

He remembered his father talking about how he could work on the farm there and how much pleasure that brought him. He also remembered how golden his father's face appeared from the days spent in the sun, without benefit of anything more than a cap with a small brim that he liked to periodically turn from one side to the other as he would walk and talk with them on those days that they visited him.

He knew that his father was not happy during those stays in the hospital, but being there seemingly gave his father some basis for remaining in this world. Whenever he saw his father both at the hospital and at the times he was at home with the family, his father always wanted to know how he was doing in school. That question became a prime motivator for him wanting to go to college and to become a rich and famous person of some kind.

His father was quite dapper in his dress, and the way he walked always made him think of men from his neighborhood who always dressed, walked, and talked as if they were always headed to nightclubs for the evening to find some pretty ladies to entertain them. Of course, when the pictures were taken at the clubs that were later brought home to verify and validate the good times had at the clubs, all of the ladies in the photos would be wearing hats and sitting in a manner that always showed legs that were crossed and strangely alluring no matter the angle from which they were being viewed. And all of the men in the pictures who wore hats would have them cocked to the side in some manner to give them the appearance of being streetwise and self-assured.

He was often sad about his father being in and out of a mental institution for most of his early life. But as a young man, he had decided early on that everyone in the world was crazy and that the same was true of every group. So, at some point in his early life, he concluded that every individual and every group had two choices: Live in your own craziness or live in somebody else's craziness. Early on, he recognized that those were not mutually exclusive options.

He understood that sometimes he would have to live in other people's craziness, if only for a moment or minute or more. And he also understood that his people (and other people) would have to live in the craziness of other groups, if only for a year or decade or century or millennium or more.

Indeed, it was in his own craziness and the craziness of his people that he found relief from the noise of various kinds that surrounded him on a daily basis. Often when he thought about his life and what was ahead for him, he thought he could be either a monk or a pimp. But he realized that neither of those was a real option. In both instances, the real obstacle was simply that he loved and adored women too much— especially the ones who had surrounded and nurtured him in his prime.

He did not cry at his father's funeral, either. He had interpreted that as being primarily related to what he thought his father might want under those circumstances: stoicism and manliness. When he accompanied his family on a small boat to witness his father's ashes being scattered on the waters of Lake Michigan not too far from where he lived at the time, he wondered why his father had made the request to be cremated and have his ashes scattered to the winds. His only belief concerning his father's death was that his father had wanted to return to the South and farm the small piece of land that his father owned in Helena, Arkansas.

He was never able to learn a lot about his father, and not a single picture of his father ever surfaced during the 60 some odd years he inhabited this earth. He always thought that was strange since he had seen pictures of his mother, his grandmother, his grandmother's brother and sister, and his mother's sister and brothers. At one point or another, he had met almost all of the people on his mother's side.

When asked about his parents, his father's reply was always: "Some young Black man and some old White woman." His father never talked about having siblings, and so everyone assumed that he did not have any. It was also speculated that the absence of siblings in his father's life was one of the causes of his mental illness and a major reason why he chose to have fifteen children.

Gregory never believed either of these ideas about his father, primarily because his father had so little interaction with any of the children except to direct and discipline them about matters related to household chores and to inquire about progress in school.

His father always walked with his hands in his pocket, and he had an air about him that said, "Don't bother me." He smoked Camel cigarettes, and his fingertips were dark with a yellow nicotine coating. He talked a lot with his hands, so Gregory had a chance to observe the dark stains of nicotine and the fact that he had one finger missing on his left hand. His father had several explanations about how that happened, but he never felt that any of the explanations given were accurate. He often wondered if his father knew what happened or cared to tell.

His father loved to wear overalls because that meant he could stand, walk, or sit and have a place to put his hands or fingers in a comfortable resting place (and perhaps to keep his missing finger from being noticed). His father also loved the out-of-doors; despite a real dislike for the cold weather and snow he had to endure as a result of his decision to follow his wife and mother-in-law to Chicago. He learned to walk briskly in the cold winters of Chicago, and it became so automatic that he would even walk fast during the summer.

In the summer months, Gregory would often sit on the back steps of the family's second-floor apartment and watch the traffic pass on Wentworth Avenue, a half-block west of his house that he could see because there were two vacant lots behind his house, one on LaSalle and the other on Wentworth.

At first, he did the traffic watching in imitation of his grandmother, but he grew to like it as a way of escaping the overcrowded and noisy apartment. His father must have seen a bit of himself in him because he would come and sit with him on this single, cold, concrete slab and ask him about how things were going with him.

As far back as he could remember, he thought he was his father's favorite child and the future for all that his father wanted to be but did not have the education or opportunity to be. From elementary school through college, almost all of the exchanges between him and his father centered on his progress in school.

There were times when his father would openly weep and tell him how proud he was of what he was accomplishing in school. And on those occasions, his father would put his arm around his shoulders and embrace him. Those were the only times his father touched him, except on those few occasions when his mother pushed his father to mete out corporal punishment for the day in relationship to some wrongdoing that she was witness to but not inclined to deal with.

What did his father do or talk about at other times? Not much. He had this sense that if his father had had a choice, he might have been a monk: speaking only when it was necessary and pursuing a life of the mind without hesitation or reservation. He even speculated that that might also be the source of his own thoughts about possibly being a monk. Where the notion came from that he might be a pimp was never clear to him, although he thought his love for women might be one source for that notion.

No one ever told him this, but he believed his father longed for the land. In Chicago, his father was able to periodically get jobs in factories, but he was never happy. He always felt that if his father could go back to Arkansas and farm, his life would have been totally different. The only time he remembered his father being somewhat content was when he got a job (through the local precinct captain) working at Chicago beaches and parks picking up paper and other debris with a little stick that had a nail on the end of it.

That was his opportunity to be outside, and he liked doing that. He lost that job after a little less than a year. The family never talked about how that happened, but it took his father to the lowest point he had ever seen him. He drank more, smoked more, and began fighting his mother, who now had a job in a paint factory.

Some of his older sisters and brothers would have to threaten to collectively jump on his father before he would leave his mother alone. His brothers and sisters thought his father was fighting his mother because she had a job and he didn't. Gregory never quite saw it that way. He always thought his father blamed his mother for them having moved from the South and, consequently, them being in their present predicament. That was what his anger was about, and his mother having a job was just a constant reminder to him that he should not have allowed her to determine the direction for the family's future.

That situation became the context for his father's search for a church in which he could be comfortable. For more than six years, his father would try a different church each month to see if there was a god to ease his pain. He finally settled in a small storefront church called Unity on 43rd and Michigan.

Gregory would learn later that Unity was pretty much unheard of in the black community at that time, but it would be the etiology for a megachurch on the South Side a half-century later. It was generally a Baptist, Lutheran, or Episcopalian church that you went to, and, rarely, you might find a Catholic church to attend if you were Black and lived on the South Side at that time.

Gregory was more comfortable at Unity than any other church the family had attended, and, in later years, he felt his father had picked that church mostly because he thought it was a good place for him to be nurtured. Despite what Unity could give his father, it could not give his father what he wanted most: a return to Arkansas with his family and a chance to be close to the land.

On one of those evenings when he sat with his father on the back porch on the cold concrete slab that was a step down to the wood porch, his father told him about how hard it was to work on the farm that his family owned back in Arkansas.

But shortly after that lengthy description of the hard work on the farm, his father would break out laughing and smiling as he transitioned to tales of how good it felt to smell the soil fresh off the morning dew. And how he rejoiced when the wind and rain would come some days and made him think of how good it felt to be alive and part of nature's grand exposition of smells, sights, and sounds of the land.

It was rare for a Black man to own property in that part of the South, but family lore had it that his father had been given the land by the father of "some old White woman" who was the mother that his father never knew. The circumstances that allowed his father's mother and father to enter into a sexual liaison were part of the family's lore that had many variations on a theme.

One of the tales surrounding the liaison was that the White woman, at the age of twenty-three, had spotted his grandfather working in the cotton fields near the big house and had decided she would get some of that. So, she arranged to have the field hand become her personal bodyguard, which allowed them to have many opportunities to be alone and together.

Another tale of how his father's mother and father got together was that his grandfather was a houseboy from the age of ten and that his grandmother and grandfather had long been friends before they had consensual sex at the age of twenty-two or twenty-three.

Although his grandfather was sent to a small town in Arkansas not far from Memphis, Tennessee after his grandmother became pregnant; his grandmother's father, at the behest of the daughter, kept in contact with the man who was the father of his grandchild. That was how his father inherited the land that he so much wanted to return to.

Chapter Three
Not to Exist

The death of his grandmother was the first time he consciously attempted to understand what it meant to not exist on this earth anymore. It was strange not to have her with the family in the kitchen on Sunday directing each child to take responsibility for preparing some part of the Sunday meal.

He remembered that all of the children in the family had to start with a small task when they were first learning how to cook under his grandmother's tutelage. Initially, the task might be as simple as greasing the cake pan and shaking a thin layer of flour over the grease to keep the cake batter from sticking.

Later on, you might be given a task as difficult as taking a cut of beef and making the entire meal of pot roast and vegetables from it.

Although his grandmother would have every child in the house working in the kitchen every Sunday; after she died, he recognized that he didn't know his grandmother very well. He knew from brief family conversations that she had been born of mixed ancestry (Indian and African American parents) somewhere in Mississippi in the nineteenth century. She had then moved to Tennessee with his mother and later came with his mother and father to Chicago.

His mother worked most of the time that his grandmother was alive, so his grandmother was his mother for the first ten or twelve years of his life, yet she never seemed real. She had an almost otherworldly existence in his mind, and beyond the preparation of the Sunday meal, almost all of his memories of her were of someone who was just there, supporting and directing his life in ways he did not fully understand.

Later in life, when he thought about how he would sit for hours on the back porch on a single, cold, stone step and watch the traffic on Wentworth Avenue go by, he realized he was imitating, in some way, his grandmother who would sit in a rocking chair on the back porch and say and do nothing for hours.

To him, she did not appear to be unhappy, but there was nothing to suggest that she was happy. She was just there. Being. Not being. And then she would return to them, giving directions for maintenance of the house in terms of chores or assistance with preparation of the meal before the arrival of his mother from work.

When his grandmother got sick and died, he had this sense of her leaving him, but he did not understand what that meant. For weeks she had been on the sofa bed in the living room, with periodic visits from Dr. Beasley, who would give her medicine to comfort her. One late afternoon during the time when she was sick, she called him to her bedside and whispered in his ear: "Keep your focus after I am gone. You will have many temptations and distractions, but you will do well if you stay focused. I will be around to help you and the family even after I shed this earthly shell."

His grandmother passed away that evening just as the family finished eating dinner and shortly after he went to check on her. She waved her hand twice to signal to him that she wanted everyone in the house to gather around her. When they all stood at her bedside, she smiled and waved one time and exhaled quietly. Dr. Beasley arrived a short time later and pronounced her dead.

The doctor routinely completed and signed the death certificate and asked the family if they had a choice of a particular funeral parlor to come and get the body. The family chose

Unity, a funeral parlor with the same name as that of the family church but completely unaffiliated with the church. Because Unity was located on 41st and Michigan, less than three-quarters of a mile from where the family lived; on the day of the funeral, the family opted to walk as a group to the funeral parlor—a sort of funeral cortege without the body.

He missed his grandmother sorely, but he had a sense that she was still always there watching over him and his family. His grandmother's other children lived not too far from where he lived, and he and a few of his siblings would often walk a few blocks over to 37th and Federal to visit Uncle Herman, who looked as if he could be the father of one of his older brothers.

His other uncle, Uncle Willie, lived farther south in Englewood and ran a grocery store on the corner of 63rd and Stewart. During the summer, Uncle Willie would pay him to come and work in the store a few hours a day so that his wife, Aunt Mae, who had developed some kind of illness, could spend less time working in the store.

The knowledge and skills that he acquired working in his uncle's store in Englewood would later help him to get a job near his house working in a grocery store that he could see from the back porch of his family's apartment. That job not only gave him spending money but it also helped him to expand his view of the world and ability to interact with people more comfortably. That job gave him his first real and sustained thoughts about women and sex and stuff like that.

During the second week of work at the grocery store near his house, he was given an order to fill and deliver to a voluptuous woman who lived on 38th and Wentworth, about a block away from the store. He had passed the three-story building where she lived many times because his post as a school safety patrol boy was on the same block. The first time that he delivered groceries to the woman, he noticed that her apartment had very subdued lighting and jazz playing in the background.

She offered him dinner and a soda, but he politely said, "No thanks, ma'am. I have to get back to the store and deliver more groceries." She took his hand and placed two single dollar bills in it, leaned over and kissed him on the cheek, and pulled him gently into her ample breasts for a moment.

As he left her apartment, his immediate thoughts were about the money she had given him. After that, however, he realized that he had an erection that exceeded anything that he had had before. He knew that this new thing that he had was in part due to his view of Ms. Belden's fabulous body, but it was also due to a slight, sweet, pleasant odor from her vagina that had aroused him in a way that he had not known before and would not know again soon.

Each time after the first time that he delivered groceries to Ms. Belden's place, she always appeared to want to have sex with him. But as soon as she would take his hand and gently pull him towards her bedroom, she would quickly drop his hand and appear to be staring at some apparition that he could not see but could feel. She would then step back and hand him the usual two dollars, smile, and wave goodbye.

It took him a while to learn what that was about. However, one evening, unexpectedly, Mrs. Belden revealed to him that whenever she attempted to enter into a sexual encounter with him, his grandmother would appear and block her way. She said she knew it was his grandmother because she met and saw her in the neighborhood before she died.

He was okay with that turn of events. The young girls in his neighborhood and school provided enough attention for him to have an outlet for his growing sexual desires. Still, there were times over the years before he went to college and the armed services that he would wake up and find his underwear and bedding totally messed up because he had dreamt about having sex with Ms. Belden. He was embarrassed, of course, when that happened, but he always felt such relief in those moments.

As he got older, he would ask himself, *Would I have enjoyed an actual encounter with Ms. Belden as much as I did in my dreams?* Of course, there was no way of answering that question, but just asking the question always made him feel alive and vibrant.

He continued to deliver groceries to Ms. Belden during the time he was in high school and working at the store, but he never feared being harmed by her. He always felt like a man when he was in the presence of Ms. Belden, and he always felt the presence of his grandmother on those occasions, too.

So, on those days that he took groceries to Ms. Belden's place, there was always a double pull that he felt in his mind and heart. On the one hand, he rejoiced at seeing Ms. Belden, and his heart would beat wildly for a long time. On the other hand, he was always inclined to behave because he thought his grandmother was around somewhere.

He was also inclined to be a loner, although he had lots of friends at school and in the neighborhood. After work on the weekend, especially on days when it was warm, he would often sit on the stoop in front of his family's apartment house and just watch the activities of the neighborhood.

He was always excited by the variety of things that went on in his neighborhood in plain sight: girls jumping double Dutch; boys playing various sports; the policy man making his evening rounds; and the frequent appearance of "chicken man"—an almost mythical figure who appeared in his neighborhood for a time that lasted well into his adulthood.

As a young man, Gregory also recalled the movements of his older brothers and sisters who would Bop, Cha-Cha, Walk, and Slow Dance—in their house, neighborhood street parties on warm summer nights, and at family gatherings in a variety of places. He would try to imitate what he saw in those places and on those occasions, but he did not learn to dance in a way that allowed him to have a true aesthetics of dance until he was in his sophomore year of high school.

At the beginning of that year of high school, his sister casually said to him, "We are going to the Friday Night Social in the gym at Phillips. Why don't you come with us? We will show you how to dance."

He had been sitting on the stoop in front of the building where he lived thinking about and pining over a girl who had broken his heart by leaving him to become the boyfriend of a senior who wanted to take her to the military ball that prior school year. He eagerly said yes to his sister's invitation, and he quickly changed clothes to join them that evening.

As they walked the six blocks to the school that early autumn evening, he felt himself skip a few times, at which his sister and her two friends chuckled. They had not seen him do that, so they asked why. His reply was, "I don't know. That's how I feel. Thank you so much for the invitation to join you. As you teach me to dance, I want you to know ahead of time that I am kind of slow; but once I got it, I got it." He smiled, and the young ladies laughed at his bit of double-talk.

The gym at Phillips was packed that warm autumn evening, and Gregory was surprised to see so many people in the place. There were students from both his school and other schools in the city. He could readily pick out two groups of fellows in the crowd: Gousters and Ivy Leaguers. The Gousters (some say the word is a Chicago variant of "Gangsters" but there are other versions of the etymology of the word) wore pointed-toes shoes, often in two colors, with pleated pants and colorful shirts with long pointed collars, and wide-brimmed hats—often turned down in the front but also worn turned up all the way around.

The Ivy Leaguers wore oxblood shoes and straight-legged pants with buttoned-down collar shirts with straight ties and bow ties. The Ivy Leaguers did not often wear hats but wore caps of various kinds. Years later, Gregory would see life-like images and examples of Gousters and Ivy Leaguers in the movie "Cooley High."

Gregory's sister told him that the first thing he had to do was be confident and self-assured, no matter what dance he was doing. She also told him to smile but not show a lot of teeth while he was dancing. She then told her friend Shirley to show him how to two-step.

That was an easy dance to learn because his ex-girlfriend had started to teach him how to do that at a party she had invited him to in the first week of his freshman year of high school. "The Glory of Love" by The Five Keys was the record that started to play, and he took Shirley in his arms and moved slowly to the music emanating from the huge speakers at the south end of the gym.

At the end of the dance, Shirley walked him over to his sister and other friends. She said proudly, "Not bad. Not bad at all, Gregory. In fact, you were pretty good at it."

He grinned and said to his sister, "I want to learn to Bop now. Geraldine seems to be good at that. Geraldine, why don't you dance with me on the next Bop record?"

The four of them stood and talked through the plays of a few other records, and then "Money Honey" by Clyde McPhatter & The

Drifters came on. Gregory took Geraldine's hand and moved to the dance floor.

She told him to focus on the music instead of her moves or his feet. He did that, but he still felt somewhat awkward. By the end of the record, he started to smile in the manner that his sister had told him. However, this was not a pretend or forced smile. He felt good about what he had been able to do.

For the rest of the evening, he stood in a corner of the gym and watched his sister and her friends move gracefully to the music with fellows who could dance well. Occasionally, he would practice alone in the corner some of the steps that Geraldine had shown him and what he thought was a good imitation of some of the fellows dancing with his sister and her friends.

Towards the end of the evening, he caught the eye of a pretty young lady who had been watching him off and on for a good portion of the evening. He had not been much inclined to dance because he still felt a little bit uncertain of his dance moves, but an instrumental tune by Earl Bostic called "Flamingo" and the young lady's pretty and coy smile gave him the courage to go over to her and ask her to Two-Step with him. When he returned her to the spot where she had formerly stood, he noticed a young lady who was a long-time friend of his smiling at him and his dance partner.

His friend said, "Oh! You two know one another?"

He replied, "No. We have not officially met or seen each other before tonight."

His friend, Charlotte, said: "Gregory, this is Francis. Francis, this is Gregory."

As the trio stood and talked in that slightly remote corner of the gym, "Dedicated to the One I Love" by The 5 Royales started to play. Without excusing herself to Charlotte or asking permission from Gregory to dance with him, Francis took his hand and led him to the dance floor. Gregory was grinning at Francis taking the initiative to get them to dance, but by the end of the dance, he was enchanted by this young lady who had to be at least one or two years older than he was.

They were leaving the dance floor when Faye Adams' "Shake a Hand" started to play, and he gently took her hand and returned with her to the dance floor. Impetuously, he nibbled on Francis' left earlobe, and her body shook for a moment. She just said to him, "Not bad," and pulled him closer to her.

When they got back to the spot where they had stood, Charlotte was smiling broadly and finally got out, "Y'all doing something bad out there?" And then she let out a hearty belly laugh. Francis got in Charlotte's face, simply smiled, and said, "Yes. Yes." At which they all laughed. They then grabbed each other's hands to leave the gym. That song had been announced as being next to the last song of the evening, so he knew he needed to find his sister and her friends to tell her about his revised plans for the evening, which he had not discussed with either Francis or Charlotte.

When he found his sister, he simply said to her that he was going to leave with Charlotte (another friend of his sister) and Francis (who was a friend of Charlotte but not known to his sister). He also told his sister that he and Charlotte would first see that Francis got home safely, and then he would walk with Charlotte to the Wentworth Gardens Housing Project just one block west of their house. He added that he shouldn't be later than midnight getting home. His sister gave him a knowing smile and then simply said, "Okay."

Francis lived on 39th and Federal, about four city blocks from the school where the Friday Night Social had been held.

It was the beginning of autumn, but the weather was still delightfully warm and only slightly breezy. Gregory and the two young ladies walked down the fourteen steps in front of the school and headed west.

Charlotte took Gregory's left hand and smiled at her own brazen move. Francis took his right hand and laughed loudly. She then kissed him on the cheek as if to mark a spot that might be interpreted as her establishing her claim on Gregory. Gregory held each young lady's hand firmly but gently. They moved synchronously down the crowded sidewalk until they had reached Federal Street. They then decided to grab each other by the waist without ever talking about it.

As they stood in front of Francis' house, a full moon emerged from behind the clouds, and the street took on an eerie glow that quickly changed to a calm and warm glow. Nobody spoke, and they just stood on the sidewalk holding one another by the waist and looking south to several sets of tracks a few blocks down.

The door to Francis' house opened, and her father stepped out on the porch, waved, and spoke to them. Her father immediately turned around and went back into the house, but he left the door open for Francis, who quickly pecked Charlotte and Gregory on the cheek and ran in the opened door.

As soon as the door was closed, Charlotte said, "Oh, you really like Francis."

Gregory smiled coyly and replied, "Yea. I like her style. She's cool!"

Charlotte was not at all surprised at that response, but she was a little chagrined by Gregory's quick and arrogant response. She thought to herself, *I have always liked this boy, but we could never get a romantic thing going. I wonder what that is about. I'm an attractive young lady. I am bright and witty. I can dance pretty well. I got style. Hmmm.*

Just as she had finished that thought, they were standing in front of her house on 39th and Wentworth. She was tempted to have a conversation about why they never developed a romantic relationship, but she decided that this may not be the best time. Still, she impetuously kissed him in the mouth and quickly turned around and entered her house without a word.

Gregory stood for a moment and thought about what had just happened. He and Charlotte had known one another since 1st grade. They both were always at the top of the class in all areas. He was the cute, charming, athletic, bright boy; and she was the pretty, witty, shapely, bright girl. Although they were always competing for academic honors and social accolades, it wasn't a conscious kind of thing. They both just tried to do their best at whatever it was they were doing.

So, the competition was not between them, but rather it was within them and manifested itself outwardly as being between them.

Gregory and Charlotte never thought about it being between them and never talked about it in those terms. It was just always there. It was the elephant in the room, so to speak, and everyone except them talked about it.

By the time they entered high school, they both ran in different but overlapping circles of people. He was with the athletic-intellectual crowd, although he decided not to get into athletics of any kind in high school and worked instead after school. Charlotte ran with the snooty-intellectual crowd but kept one foot in the athletic crowd.

They often saw each other on the way to school and at gatherings of various kinds, and they would often hug and peck each other on the cheek. But things never went beyond that, although many of their mutual friends thought that there was something between them that was not being shown or talked about.

Gregory never pursued a relationship with Charlotte, but he did decide to vigorously pursue one with Francis. At first, his pursuit of Francis was tentative. He would wait to see if he could run into her and just have a few dances with her at the Friday Night Socials at Phillips. That went on for several weeks until she decided to ask him, "When are you going to try and get in my draws?"

They were standing in a dark corner of the gym at the moment Francis had asked the question, but he still answered, "Now."

And with that, he had reached under her skirt and pulled down her underwear, unzipped his pants, and tried to enter her standing up. That was exciting but awkward. They both just made themselves presentable and left the gym and went to the Audio-Visual Room on another floor. He had a key to access that space because he was President of the Audio-Visual Club.

He cleared an area on a table at the back of the room, took off his suit coat and laid it on the table, and had Francis lay on the table on her back with her legs spread so that he could easily slide into her. Oh, my lord! Both he and Francis realized that their activities in the Audio-Visual Room were being discovered after hearing several rounds of knocking at the door. They did not answer, and the knocking stopped after several minutes.

They pulled themselves together, put their ears next to the door to see if they could hear anything, and then quickly exited the room and the area where the room was located. They managed to return to the gym without being noticed and stood near the north end of the bleachers smiling. Francis finally said, "You are crazy!"

Gregory responded, "Well, I guess that makes two of us."

They danced a few more times, watched their friends acting silly, and then just left the gym and the school a short time before it was all to end. That was the beginning of a long relationship between them that evening. They both always enjoyed their being together despite them both having involvement with other people that was decidedly more romantic but not nearly as exciting and satisfying sexually as the one they had over several years.

Chapter Four
Grace and Beauty

When he finally went off to college at the young age of 17, he had thought about wanting to be a chemist. After one semester of studying hard in that field, he left the college he attended in a nearby state and returned home to attend a local institution.

When he enrolled in the local college, he had decided that he did not want to be a chemist. What he couldn't decide was what else he might be. He took a bunch of liberal arts or general courses after he returned to Chicago. One of the courses that he took that semester was "European History from WWI to 1950."

That course was taught by a short, brilliant, Jewish professor who had to stand on a box to be easily seen by students in the huge lecture hall. The early lectures in the course were fairly interesting. But when the professor got to the part of the course related to Hitler and the rise of the Nazis in Germany, he would stand on the box that he used behind the lectern, and then to get a little more height, he would stand on his tiptoes, lean forward, raise his voice, and wildly bang on the lectern with his fist whenever he wanted to be emphatic about something. After several times of being a witness to this dramatic exposition of history, Gregory knew that he wanted to major in history.

He now had a focus for his work in college, but he quickly understood that he did not have the necessary money to complete college. He finished that second semester of college and rushed off to join the Army, see the world, and acquire funds that would allow him and millions of men like him to finish college and take America to a new and more prosperous level in its evolution as a world democracy and world power.

His first stop in the Army was at Fort Carson, Colorado, where he spent eight weeks in arduous training that all recruits had to endure. His next sixteen weeks were spent in training at Fort Benjamin Harrison near Indianapolis, Indiana. After that training, to be a military stenographer, he was shipped to Germany for the next two and a half years.

When he arrived in Germany in 1958, Charlie Parker had been dead for three years as a result of a heroin overdose; Emmett Till, a young Black boy from Chicago's South Side, had been murdered three years earlier by two White men in Mississippi; and Till's death provided the initial spark for the Civil Rights Movement that had started in earnest three years earlier when Rosa Park refused to give up her seat to a White bus rider because she had thought about Emmett Till at that moment she was being told to move to the back of the bus.

The time that he had spent overseas in the Army was more exciting and liberating than he had anticipated. He was able to travel all over Europe; enter into moving relationships with a variety of women; finish two years of college at the University of Maryland's overseas branch; and earn money to complete his college education through the G.I. Bill from the federal government and tuition assistance from the state government. He also met and became engaged to a pretty young woman after he returned home from Germany.

The woman that he met and wanted to marry was stunning in terms of appearance. However, he would soon see that she was a liar. She was not just a liar. She was a beautiful liar. That is what kept them together for all those years. And even after they parted ways, he had mostly fond memories of her and the times and love they shared. Part of what he thought about her is that all people lie, for one reason or another. Her problem was that she was a pathological liar who told lies even when it was unnecessary. He often wondered if she knew when she was lying or when she was telling the truth.

When they first met, he was not sure why he felt such an attraction towards Grace. She was an attractive woman, but there was much more to what he felt for her other than her beauty. They were making love one evening with Charlie Parker playing in the background, and in the middle of their lovemaking, she told him, "Lydia, Bird's love interest when he was here in Chicago, is my mother." She went on to tell him that Parker had a sadness about him that her mother always saw disappear after they made love in her luxurious apartment on Oakwood Boulevard off of South Parkway.

Grace added, "Each time after they made love, Parker could play the sax in a way that he had wanted to, but it took him a long time to fully master the technique. Over many months, he realized that if he combined some techniques that he had only tried in isolation, he could get the sound he had only felt and imagined for years.

"When he thought he was ready for a bigger stage than Chicago, he decided to go to New York. He offered to take my mother with him, but my mother decided she wanted to stay here in Chicago. She also decided that she wanted to leave 'the life' and settle down with a gentleman who became my father."

Gregory and Grace never got married, and he was never sure how they even became engaged. Probably on a whim emanating from some sweet moment they both found exhilarating. He knew he loved Grace, and he was sure that she loved him. But there had always been a little tension in their relationship that he could never quite understand.

During the times that they tried to discuss what they obviously both felt, they never got to what was the real issue. Often, they would just literally walk away and return to each other when the time felt right. After a couple of years of walking away from one another, he decided to walk away from her for good. It wasn't that he didn't love her, but he always felt that she had a shadow hiding in her heart somewhere.

He had never been the kind of dude you would see hanging out alone on a Friday or Saturday night. Neither was he the kind of dude you would see hanging with his boys on a Friday or Saturday night. His preference was always to have a woman on his arm when he went out to have a good time on the weekend or any other day of the week for that matter.

And it wasn't because he was afraid to be alone. He had a propensity to want to be alone even when he was in the company of others. That propensity was probably what allowed him to believe that he could be a monk and what pushed him away from Grace with only a little bit of regret.

In his late adolescence and early adulthood, he had another propensity that had pushed itself to the forefront of his being as a young Black man from the South Side of Chicago: The propensity to want to be in the company of women; especially brilliant, graceful, well-endowed, and beautiful women. That was probably what pulled him towards Grace.

He understood that part of his desire to be with women came from his love for his grandmother, but there was another layer to that desire that even he did not fully understand. While most of the other young men in his neighborhood spent most of their time fooling around and playing—at life, love, and working—he always had a legitimate hustle: for knowledge, money, and women— other terms for beauty and grace in his world.

Chapter Five
Swank and Swagger

Even as a young man at Roosevelt University in Chicago in the early 1960s, Gregory had started to acquire a hustle and swagger that attracted women and alienated men, or at least made them envious. He never understood why any man would be envious of another man. That just never made sense. He always thought: *Create your own swagger and hustle, whatever that is or may be.*

His first hint of the trouble that his hustle and swagger might cause him came when he took a history course at the university with an instructor who had just finished his doctorate in history at DePaul University in Chicago. The instructor was an articulate man with a good knowledge of his subject. But he did not like to be questioned about anything he said, and Gregory naively thought that's what his role was in the class: to ask questions and offer points of view different from what was in the book or being said by the instructor.

That was a mistake. The instructor soon made it clear that he was the only source of knowledge in that course, and he would turn red whenever a student raised his hand and said anything that seemed to question either what was in the book or being said by the instructor, who appeared to be especially infuriated by anything said by Gregory in the course. When he got a "C-" for a midterm grade and approached the instructor about it, the instructor told him that he was just "too goddamn arrogant." When he asked for clarification about what had been said, the instructor said: "You come to class all dressed up, you walk into the class as if you own it, and you engage with the women as if they were part of your harem. Who in the fuck do you think you are?"

He was shocked by what had been said to him, and, initially, he thought that he was being confronted by overt racism for the first time in his life. He hesitated before he replied. Then he said, "You don't like me because I am Black."

The instructor sheepishly looked down and then up at him and said, "No. You being Black has nothing to do with it. I don't like you because you are an articulate, well-dressed, good-looking son of a bitch!"

At that moment, he saw his instructor for the first time: He was a short, pale, overweight, average-looking man at whom you would not give a second glance if you saw him on the street. In addition, his sense of aesthetics in terms of attire was outside the box: Pale yellow shirt and pale-yellow tie; brown single-breasted suit with pants without a cuff; tan shoes and green socks. One could almost get the effect he was going for in terms of dress, but he had missed the mark.

He left his instructor's office without saying another word, went to a nearby bar to have a beer, and made the decision that he would neither drop nor return to that history class. He did not care if he flunked the course, but for some reason, he got a "C" for a final grade. He never again saw the instructor's name associated with a course at the university, and he never inquired about what might have happened to him.

In that encounter with the instructor, the lesson that he learned was simple: being in the world in the way that he wanted would probably bring him joy from women and envy from men. But that encounter with the instructor gave him something else that was just as important. It helped him understand why Blacks were always saying that racism just drove them crazy: Blacks were always having confrontations with individuals from other races or ethnic groups, but they could never be sure what the confrontations were really about!

Gregory understood that conflicts and confrontations between individuals and groups had probably always been part of the human condition, but as a Black person, your first and immediate response was one often filtered through the lens of racism. And, often, that would be the correct choice of lens. In this instance, it turns out, that was not the correct lens, and for some reason, that error gave him the freedom to move about in the world with a little more ease.

Things got better at the university after that first semester. He even found a job at the United States Post Office to supplement the money he got from the federal and state governments because he had been a GI. Now, of course, he had the means to take his hustle and swagger to another level, which he did.

After a final year at Roosevelt University and receipt of his degree in history, he was assigned to the staff of a local high school, which had a reputation for crime and gang violence. Although he had attended a high school a little more than a mile north of the place he had now been assigned, he had some trepidation about his new assignment because that high school had always had a reputation for being a rough and tough place that kept students from being able to focus on their academics, and this was especially true after the Robert Taylor Housing Project was completed in the late 1950s.

His initial assignment was in the Upper-Grade Center of the high school, which essentially was an attempt to place 9th-grade students in an environment close to other students but still administratively and physically apart from other grades in the high school. He could never decide if that concept was a good one or a bad one. Like many other ideas for school reform in the inner-city of most large American cities, it was not based upon any good theoretical or pragmatic reasons for instituting change.

Although he had some concerns about his new assignments, in many ways, it was a good fit. He understood a lot about the lifestyle of young people at the school because he was young and from the South Side of Chicago. He had an instant comfort when interacting with students that soon gave him the reputation of being a good teacher and a nice guy and a moniker that followed him for the length of his stay at the school: Supercool.

At the Upper-Grade Center, the principal liked him for the way he handled his classes and his interactions with students in the halls and other places in the school. But at the end of his first year of teaching, at the request of the district superintendent, he had been transferred to the 10-12 grade division of the high school. He never understood why he was chosen for that assignment, but he had another level of comfort because the programming administrator had given him United States History as his major subject to teach. That course was taken only by juniors and seniors.

When the programming administrator talked to him about his course assignments, she said, "I have given you one of the most sought-after courses to teach because I think you can handle the students and the subject matter. However, so that you do not appear to be given some kind of preferential treatment, I have also given you two sections of the least sought-after course in your department: Civics I."

The programming administrator paused, smiled, and continued by saying, "This will be your most difficult course to teach because only 10th graders who are slow take this course. However, coming from the Upper-Grade Center, you should do well. Right?"

His reply was simply, "Yes, ma'am."

The programming administrator smiled at his reply and said, "I will give you advanced placement classes next year if you can handle well your class assignment this year. Deal?"

This time he smiled and replied, "Yes, ma'am."

He trusted the programming administrator, but his initial and gut reaction was a feeling that he had just made a deal with the devil. He did not fully understand his reaction until the end of his last class on the first day of school. He was standing in front of the class after cleaning the chalkboard, and when he turned around, one of his female students continued to sit and stare at him.

He said, "Young lady, how can I help you?"

She replied, "The better question is, how can I help you?"

He was somewhat shocked by her answer but quickly replied, "Say some more."

She seemed surprised by his response but coyly smiled and replied: "I am only sixteen, but I am a woman who has had experiences with men twice my age and older. I can help you experience sex in ways that you will never forget."

He raised his eyebrows at that comment and said, "Really?"

He then told her to stand up and come closer to him so that she would not miss a word of what he wanted to tell her. He then said, "Do you know how long it took me to get my education and credentials for this teaching job? Do you know how much money it took to get my education and credentials for this teaching job? Do you think I would risk losing this job for an opportunity to have sex with a 16-year-old girl? You don't have to respond to any of those questions, but don't ever even think about approaching me about such matters." He then just pointed to the door without saying another word.

The look on the young lady's face was one of terror, and he hated having to have that confrontation with her, primarily because he understood that part of her brazen behavior was attributable to her youth. The other part of her brazen behavior was attributable to responses she had probably received from the outside world.

After that encounter, the school year went extremely well, and there were some days when he felt good about being a teacher. Apparently, the word got around that he was not up for playing games with students, and he absolutely was not up for fooling around with female students. Despite friendly smiles and flirtatious looks in class and in the halls and invitations to dance on social occasions in the school, the female students kept a respectable distance from him physically and in their conversations.

The real problem started to come from female staff members in his department and then from other departments in the school. The female that finally caught his eye was from the business department at the school. She had this huge afro that was fashionable at the time and that framed a gorgeous face that usually displayed an infectious smile. He ignored her at first, but he finally decided to sit at her table, where she usually ate alone in the teachers' lunchroom.

He got directly to the point by saying, "I am Gregory, and I would like to get to know you better."

She did not crack a smile or say anything for a few seconds, but she finally said, "I know who you are, and I know your reputation here in the school with the ladies. My name is Sharon. We will see about you getting to know me better. There is a party this Friday at my friend's house. Why don't you come to the party? My class is about to start so I will get more information to you later today. Goodbye."

He continued to sit as she rose and took her food tray to a rack for cleaning. He had not seen her walk away from him before, and he smiled broadly at her curvaceous body and beautiful legs as she exited the lunchroom. He tried to think about what he would say to her when he saw her again, but all of what he could think about at that moment seemed trite or boyish. He switched to thinking about what he would do in the class he had coming up the next period.

When he saw her at the party given at her friend's house that Friday, he marveled at her beauty and the ease with which she navigated the party. She hugged individuals and chatted with others as if she were the hostess of the party. And in some sense, she was. It was her party given at a friend's spacious apartment in the South Shore neighborhood just off of the lake and 67ᵗʰ Street.

The party had gotten started by the time he arrived, so he jumped into it without even taking off his coat. "Heat Wave" by Martha & The Vandellas was playing, and he grabbed a young lady by the hand who was standing by the door and pulled her up real close to him with his right hand on his right side and leaned in on her body. This was always his signature move when he was Bopping, and he held the young lady longer than usual. She smiled at that move and turned around quickly to show him her shapely legs. The rest of that dance could have easily been sexual foreplay; but when the song was finished, he thanked the young lady and bowed. She smiled at that gesture and bowed back.

He gave his coat to a person who was checking coats, looked again at the young lady he had danced with walking away from him, and exhaled at the sight of her floating out of sight. She was dazzlingly cute, petite, and curvaceous. And she could dance well! His impulse was to see if she would go home with him immediately, but he wanted to see Sharon and see who else and "what else" might be at the party.

He glanced around the room to see who else he knew. The crowd was a good mixture of Chicago's Black bourgeoisie: teachers, lawyers, doctors, businessmen, policemen, other civil servants, writers, accountants, and a few hairstylists, one of which appeared to be getting more than his fair share of attention from Sharon. Initially, Gregory was inclined to watch the interaction between Sharon and the stylist, but he decided that he could not be jealous of anyone she interacted with. He barely knew the woman.

He turned his attention to a group of women who had gathered in an area near a window facing the north side of the city. One of the women gathered there gave him a coy smile that he responded to by raising his right hand slightly and waving to her. She nodded and moved away from the group to a more isolated area in an adjacent but still visible room. He took that at his cue to follow her.

When they reached a somewhat secluded area of the apartment and sat together on a window seat with the sun to their back, she said to him: "Are you alone or are you with someone?"

He replied, "Well, it is kind of both."

She smiled and said, "Tell me how that could be."

His reply was, "I just met Sharon, and she invited me to the party. I have expressed an interest in getting to know her, but I don't know what is going to be my relationship with her going forward."

She replied, "Oh, I see, but I don't see the two of you sharing much space or conversation. What's that about?"

His reply was, "I don't know. I just arrived. But tell me, what is your name and who are you here with?"

She replied, "My name is Karen, and I came with one of the ladies you saw me talking with near the window."

Except for Karen, he hadn't paid much attention to the ladies gathered at the window, so he smiled and said, "What other ladies?"

She laughed and said, "Cute."

They sat and bantered for the next forty-five minutes and tuned out most of what was going on around them until Sharon walked up and said, "Hello, you two. Are you having a good time?"

Gregory blushed and said, "Yes. A great time."

Karen also blushed and said, "Lovely. Lovely time."

Those responses were followed by a bit of uneasy silence until Sharon said, "Karen, I see that you and Gregory are having a good time talking to each other, but I would like to borrow Gregory for a few minutes to introduce him to some folks. Do you mind?"

Karen replied, "No, I don't mind if it is okay with Gregory."

With that response, Sharon reached out her hand to take the hand of Gregory and gently helped him stand. Holding Gregory's hand tightly, Sharon walked away from Karen and quickly looked back at her with a haughty sneer, which surprised Karen because she had always thought of Sharon as a good friend and likable person. That moment revealed something about Sharon that made Karen uneasy.

Karen continued to sit in the window seat and watch the folks in the larger room. She still had half of the gin and tonic that she had when she and Gregory had first started their conversation. And after the exchange with Sharon, she sat back in her seat a little bit more, got a cigarette and lit it, and crossed her legs to show a nice view of her inviting thighs. Karen thought to herself, *Interesting gentleman. I wonder should I pursue him, let him pursue me, or leave him alone because of Sharon?*

Chapter Six
Somewhere in The World

Gregory dutifully followed Sharon around the crowded room and was happy about the turn of events for the evening. He had two gorgeous women interested in him, and one still held his hand tightly as if to never let him go. The other one still sat in a corner of the room and watched him move through the crowd.

He turned his head briefly away from Karen when Sharon introduced him to a fellow who was a captain in the Chicago Police Department. He was a rather handsome fellow who was the husband of the woman in whose house the party was being held. When he turned back to look for Karen, she was gone. He wistfully sighed and turned back to see Sharon staring at him angrily.

He wasn't sure how to respond, so he said, "Can I get you another drink, darling?"

Sharon had not expected that response, and she smiled and said, "Yes, baby. Moet champagne."

With that exchange, Gregory headed to one of several bars in the room. He had genuinely wanted to reduce the tension he felt between him and Sharon a few minutes ago, but his offer to get her a drink was also motivated by his desire to see if Karen was still at the party. He did not see her. He returned to Sharon with a drink in each hand: Moet champagne for her and a gin and tonic for himself.

Sharon immediately said, "She's gone. Right?"

Gregory replied, "I think so. I did not see her in the room."

Sharon said, "So you got yourself a gin and tonic to try to hold on to her for a bit longer?"

Gregory hesitated, looked at the glass he still held in his hand, and then laughed and said: "I guess you are right."

Sharon just stared at him for a few minutes; then she said, "Take me home with you tonight."

He said, "Okay."

Sharon asked him to get her wrap, and she went to tell her friend that she was leaving with Gregory and going to his place. Sharon's friend just smiled and winked at that bit of information, and then she gave Sharon a hug and a squeeze of the hand.

As he and Sharon left the party, he turned his head a bit to the left because he felt someone was staring at him somewhere. It was Karen who was staring at him. She had returned to the window seat where they had previously sat together. Karen only looked at him without offering a hint about what she felt at that moment. She then just turned her head to speak to a fellow who had brought her a drink and offered it up to her at that moment.

Watching Karen interact with the gentleman who had brought her a drink helped Gregory a lot. His resolve now was to leave Karen alone and pursue Sharon aggressively. He held Sharon's hand as they left the party to go to his place. She told him to take her to her car and that she would follow him home. He nodded in assent, grabbed her around the waist, pulled her to him, and kissed her gently on the lips.

She smiled at the move and said: "Nice!"

When they reached his condominium on 52nd and Cornell in Hyde Park, he realized he had not told her that she could park in the garage in a second space that he had. Instead of entering the garage directly, he pulled up and stopped in a no-parking zone in front of the building. She had followed his lead and had parked directly behind him.

He walked up to the driver's side of her car and said, "Here is a card to get into the garage. Just stick it in the slot on the left side of the garage entrance and wait for me somewhere inside of the garage. I have a second card, and I will show you where to park once I enter the garage."

Sharon said to him, "Boy Scout!"

He replied to her, "At your service, ma'am."

As they entered his condominium, Sharon smiled and again said, "Nice!"

He replied, "Thank you. Can I get you a drink? And what would you like?"

She replied, "Well, what do you have?"

He said, "Don't you remember? I am a Boy Scout."

Sharon smiled, put her hand over her mouth, coughed quietly, and replied: "I want what you and Karen were drinking this evening. What was it? Gin and tonic with a twist of lime?"

He smiled and said, "Coming up."

Before he left to get Karen a drink, he walked across the living room and turned on the stereo. He chose a tune by the Whispers that he had not listened to for a while: "It's You." And instead of getting Sharon her drink, he put out his hand to ask her to dance with him. Neither had spoken a word at that moment, but she quickly folded herself into his arms, and he gently and gracefully moved his and her body around the room as if they were ballroom dancers.

As they danced, Sharon thought to herself: *Yes. Boy Scout and player*!

After the first Whispers' tune finished, he went to get Sharon a drink. He returned with two gin and tonic drinks and found her looking out of the window at the lake. That side of his apartment was almost all glass: To the left was a double glass door and screen that led to the balcony overlooking the park and the lake below; on the right was a long heating unit and a large window with the same view as the one from the balcony.

Although he knew she could see him in the reflection of the window, he quietly moved up behind her, held her close from behind, placed a drink in her right hand, and kissed her on the left side of her neck. She shuddered. Still, she turned towards him, kissed him in the mouth, moved away from the window to the center of the room, handed him her drink, unrobed completely, and then reached to get her drink from him. He gave her the glass, then put Barbara Mason's "Yes, I'm Ready" on the record player.

Although both knew that they might be seen from the outside even when standing away from the window, they both just sat their drinks on the cocktail table near the black and white sofa. They embraced and kissed like forlorn lovers being united after a long period of being apart.

They both now stood naked in the middle of the room with all of the lights on. Neither seemed to care. And as they continued to be serenaded by the Whispers and other R&B groups, they continued to embrace and kiss until both had started to secrete joy juice on the foot of the other. He was surprised at the amount of fluid that flowed from her body. That must have surprised her, too, because she said, "That has never happened to me before. You must have your mojo working?"

He replied, "You mean we?"

He pulled her down to the rug, gently entered her, looked away to keep his mind off of the mounting pleasure he felt, and then told her to stop, which she did immediately because she wanted him to wait for her to reach her orgasmic climax. Although he was totally into the moment, an image of Karen did flash across his mind, and he wondered what that meant both in terms of the woman he was on top of and the woman he had hoped he might be on top of earlier in the evening.

Sharon moaned a little, and he thrust deeper into her until they both were in a frenzy to get home to Jesus, which they did simultaneously. She laughed, he cried, and they briefly nodded off until his phone rang. He could not imagine who that might be, so he just ignored the ringing. When it stopped, he said: "That was good."

She replied, "Yes. That was 'real' good! Can I have some more?"

He had her play with his nipples for a few minutes, and then they were back at it with much of the frenzy they both had brought to their earlier lovemaking. There was not the urgency that dominated their earlier moments of intimacy, but this time around was even better in many ways: He could better savor the pleasure of each slow downward stroke into her without worrying about prematurely reaching an orgasm, and she could fully feel the inside of her begin to pulsate and pull him deeper into her. This time they both howled loudly.

Although they had never talked about it, he kind of knew that she would not be able to spend the night with him, so he shook her a bit and said, "How much longer can you stay?"

She replied, "About an hour longer. You know I am married, right?"

He replied, "Yea, I suspected as much, although we never talked about it. Tell me why you are out here in the streets."

She hesitated but finally said, "It's not hard to figure out. My husband is a policeman, and he spends a great deal of time away from home. Some of the time that he is away from home is related to legitimate police work, but a lot of that time is related to him playing around in the streets with other women. I heard from a reliable source that he has another woman about two blocks over from where we live."

He bowed his head slightly upon hearing that, and then he took her chin, lifted it, and turned her face so he could look into her eyes. He then said softly, "I will make it better."

He pulled her closer to him as they lay on their side on the black rug. He then turned her slightly so that he had a good view of her firm and ample breast. And then he alternated sucking each breast until he heard her emit a sound that almost magically moved him to turn her on her back and slide effortlessly into her with a heightened sense of excitement that felt like an out-of-body experience.

She shook him about an hour later to tell him that she had to leave. He got a facecloth and towel for her to clean herself, and then he showed her to the guest bathroom just off the kitchen. Before she could close the door to the bathroom to tidy up, he offered: "There are several containers of Summer's Eve under the sink if you want to freshen up a bit."

She said, "Okay," but she thought to herself: *Nope, not boy scout or player. Stone player*!

As she finished freshening up, she thought to herself, *Why am I rushing to get home? He is probably not home and will spend the night around the corner with that bitch he is spending so much time with now that I have told him I want a divorce.*

As she exited the bathroom, she told him: "You don't need to walk me to my car. I've decided to spend the night. Take your clothes off, boy."

He asked, "Boy? Or did you say Roy?"

She smiled at his joke and replied, "Actually, I meant to say Stone Player."

He laughed and replied: "Yep."

Chapter Seven
What in The World

Gregory was slightly surprised when he woke up the next morning and found Sharon naked next to him. He smiled, but he had several concerns about their relationship going forward.

His main concern was that she was still married. His other concern was about the nature of the relationship between Sharon and the hairstylist that she had given so much attention to at the party. He was tempted to wake her up and talk about the hairstylist, but he decided instead that he would make her breakfast and leave that alone for the moment.

He liked Sharon a lot, and their lovemaking was even beyond exquisite. Still, he wondered about the choice he had made. Should he have pursued Karen instead of Sharon? Sharon was married and Karen was not. Both were beautiful women with fabulous bodies. Both were intelligent and sophisticated women who knew their way around the social scene in Chicago. What was missing in either case?

He wasn't sure about the answer to that question, but as he was about to turn to place the cooked breakfast on the table, Sharon came and hugged him from behind and tenderly kissed him on the back of the neck. He shuddered, turned around with plates still in each hand, leaned down to kiss her bare breast, and trembled so much that he had to put the plates down.

Whatever previous thoughts he had about breakfast and the hairstylist were lost as he laid her on the edge of the kitchen table, continued to stand, and slid into her while looking at her full breast heave and listening to her groan with pleasure. Ahhhh.

He wasn't sure how she arranged to be away from her house, but they spent the long weekend cooking, eating, drinking, watching movies, making love, talking, and just lying around holding one another. They never left his condo.

Late on Sunday, they both recognized that they needed to get ready to go to work the next morning. He accompanied her to her car in the garage, told her to call him when she got in, and playfully reached in the open car window and fondled her breast. She playfully pushed down on the gas pedal to rev the motor. They both laughed and gingerly kissed each other goodbye.

As Sharon pulled out of the garage, he thought about the fact that he had not pursued a conversation with Sharon about the nature of her relationship with the hairstylist. He also realized that he had not thought much at all about Karen the entire weekend. Now he wondered if it was wise to continue thinking about her given the wonderful time he had spent with Sharon.

Still, he did vividly recall the moments that he had spent with Karen at the party, and he felt some regret about not being able to follow through with some kind of contact with her that evening. He did not even know how to get in touch with her now. With that thought, his regret turned into lament.

He went to work that next morning with a bit of glee that he had not known for a long time. He recognized that part of what he felt came from the ecstasy he had experienced when he and Sharon were deeply immersed in one another over the weekend. Part of what he felt, however, came from some wild thoughts he had about Karen. He knew that pursing Karen might mean trouble between him and Sharon, but Karen had an aura of lightness about her that he reveled in. He thought that she was a great counterbalance to his phlegmatic, heavy soul.

He and Sharon ate lunch together for several days in a row, with just light banter for those three early days of the week. On Thursday, without giving it much thought, he said to Sharon, "I want to get in contact with Karen. Do you have the information you can share with me to do that?"

She smiled at his question, looked into his eyes for a while, opened the notebook she had, tore out a sheet of paper, wrote Karen's name and number on the paper, handed the paper to Gregory, and said: "I appreciate the fact that you are not sneaking around behind my back in your efforts to contact Karen. I don't know why you want to contact her, but I am sure you will be as straightforward with me about that as you were about asking me for information about her. That's fair. I have a husband and children and a lover on the side that I know you have thought about. Of course, I mean the hairstylist. I love you, but I understand. Keep in touch."

Sharon exited the lunchroom without saying another word to him or taking another look at him. He did not like making her feel bad, but he thought fair was fair: she did have a husband and lover and kids. Why could he not have Karen in his life? If she would agree to such an arrangement since he would undoubtedly tell her about Sharon if she did not already know, what was the problem?

Gregory knew that men mistakenly thought that women wanted to be loved the way men thought they should love a woman; but in reality, women wanted to be loved the way women thought a man should love a woman. The same was true of women. Women mistakenly thought that men wanted to be loved the way women thought they should love men; but in reality, men wanted to be loved the way men thought they should be loved by a woman.

In both cases, neither men nor women often got what they wanted from a relationship with the opposite sex. Gregory, however, felt that

Karen could give him what he wanted in a relationship.

He had no idea about what he would do with the information Sharon had just given him. His initial thought was that he would immediately contact Karen to see if he could set up a date of some kind with her over the weekend. He hesitated about doing that because he thought that she might say "no" or reject him outright because of the way he had handled the situation at the party. And, of course, he thought about how she might respond to the idea of him still seeing Sharon. No matter! He wanted to be with Karen in the worst way, and he wasn't even sure why.

He went to a telephone in the main office and dialed the number for Karen. The phone rang, but no one answered. He hesitated and then hung up. He decided he would try to contact her after school was over; but as he headed to class, he went to the social studies department's office and dialed her number for a second time with the same results. He was now frantic about reaching her and decided to go to Sharon's classroom to seek her counsel. Since the period had started, Sharon was shocked to see him standing at her door.

She immediately inquired, "Don't you have a class now?"

Feeling somewhat ashamed in the moment, he said: "Yes, but I need your help. I have tried to reach Karen, but she is not answering. I know her shift at the hospital does not start until three. What might be the problem?"

Sharon's immediate inclination was to be mean, and she thought about telling Gregory that Karen was probably fucking another man at that time of day. Instead, she simply said, "She is off today, but she has an appointment with her gynecologist. Nothing serious. An annual checkup. You should be able to get her by the time school is out. You better hurry up to your class."

Despite making inquiries about a woman he was lusting for, he lustfully kissed Sharon in the mouth and moved quickly towards his class. That gesture seemed to have caught Sharon off guard, and she continued to stand outside of her classroom long after Gregory had disappeared. She thought to herself: *Maybe I can be in a relationship with Gregory and Karen. Sounds kind of crazy, but it might just work.*

When Gregory got to his classroom, the assistant principal was standing in front of the class teaching. He continued even after Gregory had been standing in front of the door for fifteen minutes. When the bell rang, students scattered into the halls, and Gregory stood before the assistant principal looking sheepishly.

The assistant principal said, "Bad idea to leave your class unattended. Anything could have happened, and you would have been held responsible for that. What were you thinking?

Don't give me an answer because I don't want you to lie, and if I know, I will have to discipline you unless it was a dire emergency."

Gregory quickly replied, "It won't happen again. I apologize for being so stupid in this situation."

Gregory thought to himself, *Boy, you dodged a bullet there! Good thing Walt is your friend and also a history teacher who was able to step in and take over as if that had been planned. Don't get stupid over a woman or these women.*

The next period for him was a prep period, so he gathered up his materials and went to the teachers' lounge. He started to leave immediately because the smoke was so heavy despite both windows being open.

Instead, he sat at an empty table, lit a cigarette from a nearly empty pack, and picked up the office telephone. He dialed Karen's number even though he was sure she would not answer. She didn't. He lit a second and third cigarette, an unusual move for him since he only smoked two or three cigarettes a day, and stared out the open windows.

He thought about how he had become a teacher almost totally based on his choice to major in history in undergrad school. There were not a lot of options for a job with that as a major. He did not regret that choice. He loved reading about the foibles and achievements of mankind. He also liked having to write papers for the many history courses he had taken.

He realized, however, that he needed to pursue an advanced degree in history if he wanted to have other options for employment. At that moment, he decided to apply to grad school and earn a master's in history. That decision lowered his general anxiety and his particular frantic feelings related to not reaching Karen.

As soon as he had stepped out of the school building, he went to a telephone booth nearby and called Karen. This time she did answer. She said, "Hello."

He replied, "Hi. This is Gregory. We met a few days ago at a party. I got your telephone number from Sharon. I didn't think you would mind."

She replied, "No. That's fine. How are you?"

He said, "I am good. I am calling to ask you out on a date this weekend. The Modern Jazz Quartet is in town at the London House. I think I can still get tickets. You interested?"

She paused but finally said, "Yes. I would like that. What time is the show? And can we have dinner there? My treat."

Gregory was pleased by Karen's suggestion to have dinner, and he was even more pleased by her offer to pay for dinner. He said, "Great.

I will get you around five on Friday. The show starts at eight."

She replied, "Okay. See you then."

Gregory felt as if he had hit the jackpot. He jumped up and down, ignoring the students and staff around him. Sharon saw him and surmised that he had contacted Karen, but she was surprised by his exuberance at having done so. She wanted to be angry but decided she would just go over and have a conversation with Gregory.

He was so into the moment that he had not realized that she had been standing behind him for several minutes before she finally spoke. She said, "Hello, Gregory. Good news? You were finally able to reach Karen?"

He said, "Yes. I was able to talk to her. We are going to go on a date on Friday."

She said, "And you are comfortable about telling me that and showing me how happy you are about that?"

He said, "Yes. I do love you, girl, and I want the nexus of our relationship to be transparent. How do you feel about that?"

She was so mad that she was trembling, but she managed to get out: "I am good with that. I hope you can take what you so freely give."

Sharon pivoted and left Gregory standing with a quizzical look on his face. The quizzical look had all to do with Sharon's last words. He thought to himself: *I, too, hope I can take what I so freely give.*

When Friday evening came, Gregory was suddenly nervous as he drove to pick Karen up to go to the London House. He was not sure why he was nervous. Was it the anticipation of being in her presence? Was it that he thought the evening would not go well? Did he think that he would be a babbling and bumbling idiot in her presence? Would he be too aggressive or not aggressive enough for her taste? Would he be able to get the right balance of whatever she wanted or needed to make her find him attractive enough to spend the evening with him and enjoy it?

He did not have much time to think about being nervous because she only lived a few blocks from him in Woodlawn. As he pulled up to the apartment building on 61st and Dorchester, she stepped out of the door before he could ring her bell and ask her to come down.

She looked dazzlingly beautiful in her beige, A-line coat that had a flair collar and that came down over her calves. She wore her hair pulled up into a ball at the top. As she approached the side of the car that he was now standing next to, he smiled and thought to himself: Audrey Hepburn—"Breakfast at Tiffany's." As he helped her get seated in the car, he glanced at her beautiful legs and smiled.

After telling her how beautiful she looked, he said: "I immediately thought of Audrey Hepburn and the movie 'Breakfast at Tiffany's.'"

She smiled and said, "You got exactly what I intended. You get extra points for that."

He started to be cute and ask when and for what he might use those extra points, but he just said, "Oh? Great!"

Chapter Eight
Where in The World

He had seen the Modern Jazz Quartet several times—once overseas and once in New York City. He was not sure when or how he came to embrace the group because they played a variety of music: jazz (bebop and other forms of jazz), classical, and blues.

Two of his favorite tunes were tunes that were far apart in terms of tempo: "Adagio from Concierto De Aranjuez," almost a funeral dirge; and "The Golden Striker," an up-tempo, bluesy, dance number that made you, at minimum, pat your foot and move your leg.

Gregory said to Karen, "Have you seen the Modern Jazz Quartet?"

Karen replied, "No. I have heard of them, but I have never seen them or listened to their music. What can I expect?"

He said, "For the most part, I think you can expect something different. Different and at the same time familiar. Classically trained, these musicians have decided that they could integrate various music genres into a unique and yet still familiar sound. Their range in terms of tunes is pretty wide, and even familiar tunes still pull you in emotionally in ways that they had not done before."

As he continued to talk, Karen smiled and thought to herself: *I like this dude's conversation. I have kind of underestimated his game. Now I know why Sharon kind of holds onto him tightly. But let me see what else he's got.*

Gregory pulled the car up to the sign that indicated valet parking. He rushed to get to the passenger side of the car so that he could again get a good view of her long, luscious legs. He was not disappointed. He licked his lips reflexively and thought to himself, *Ahh*.

After they entered the London House, the maitre d' inquired about checking their coats, so Gregory assisted Karen with the removal of her coat. She wore this stunning, long, black dress that did indeed make him think of Audrey Hepburn, absent the long black gloves. As he removed her wrap, he was tempted to kiss her on her bare shoulders, but he thought that move might be one for a later time in the evening.

He had been to the London House before, almost a decade ago, but he did not remember much about the place, especially the food. He thought the food was American fare. As it turned out, they had many Italian dishes, too. He had the fettuccine and scampi, and Karen had spaghetti and grilled chicken. Both simple enough dishes for individuals who made simplicity one of the themes of their life.

He tried not to stare at Karen, but that was difficult. She was even prettier than he remembered from the night he first met her at Sharon's party over near the lakefront. She had this slightly round face, ample eyebrows (not painted on!), smooth skin (almost no powder that you could see), nice full lips (muted with a soft lipstick), authentic smile (no photograph being taken this time), and a soft aura about her face.

After watching him watch her, she said, "Well? What do you think?"

He simply said, "Lovely. Lovely."

She smiled and said, "That's exactly what I was thinking about you, with a masculine notion of that word, of course."

He smiled and looked her in the eyes, but he did not respond to her comment at that moment. However, he did very much like what she had just said and the way she said it.

Before he could find words to speak, the waiter brought a pear and walnut salad that they had decided to split. It was delightful, mainly because of the pears and salad dressing (a strawberry, blush wine vinaigrette). They mostly ate in silence, talking only about the food. He thought to himself, *I hope that I do not have to choose between Karen and Sharon. They are both the kind of women I like hanging with.*

After they had finished eating, they just sat and drank champagne and cooed with each other until the band came on. He was so comfortable with Karen that he felt as if he had known her a long time. Of course, he had only known her for a few weeks. She had this presence that made him feel calm and excited at the same time. That was unusual because he usually felt one or the other with most women he knew. He could indeed be calm and excited with other women, but it was never at the same time.

He kept thinking: *What is it about Karen that makes me feel these two opposite ways simultaneously? It is a high that I have never been able to get to even with drugs.* He tried to think about how that would work, but the MC announced the group's arrival on stage.

The group's opening number, "Django," brought him fully back to the moment and made him quickly recall the time in London when he was in the service in the late 50s. He and his buddy, Pat, had flown from Heidelberg to London to see the MJQ (as they were often called back then) perform. That was his second time in London, and he vividly remembered the reception and respect that the crowd gave these Black musicians from the United States. Just recalling that moment made him a little teary-eyed.

The next tune the group played was one of his favorites: "The Golden Striker." What joy he felt in his heart as the group romped through that tune. Milt Jackson was on fire, and the rest of the group followed his lead and played with a verve that made him want to cry! The group followed that tune with numbers he was familiar with and loved: "No Sun in Venice," "Bags' Groove," "Fontessa," "Night in Tunisia," "Yardbird Suite," "Vendome," "Lonely Woman," "Willow Weep for Me," "The Jasmine Tree," "Here's That Rainy Day," "One Never Knows," and "Summertime."

He was surprised at how raucous the crowd was at the end of the last number played for that set. They were standing on their feet, clapping, whistling, shouting 'bravo,' stomping, and hollering 'MJQ' over and over again. He again thought about the crowd in London more than a decade before as they applauded the group for almost ten minutes straight.

He felt good to be alive and a witness to such beauty and grace—both in terms of the music and the men who performed the music. He also felt happy to be in the company of a woman who had the same kind of beauty and grace he had witnessed and been in the company of for most of his life.

As they left the London House, Karen had gently grabbed his arm and pulled him closer to her. She appeared to be ecstatic, and he felt it had all to do with the evening they had shared. Clearly, she wanted the evening to go on, although she had not said as much. He told her about a nightclub nearby with a DJ that played a wide variety of dance music.

She immediately said, "Let's go."

They wound up at Cockney Pride, a restaurant by day and a mixed-crowd (including gays) dance club in the evening. They sat for a while and talked until Aretha Franklin's "Chain of Fools" started to play. That was followed by several other up-tempo tunes. So, they stayed on the dance floor and grooved to them, too. At the moment that Gregory had been inclined to sit for a minute, the Delfonics' "La La La I Love You" came on. They held each other really tight on that number, and when it was over, she said: "Let's go to my place."

He said, "Okay."

As they drove away from the Cockney Pride, he was headed towards Woodlawn, but she said: "Oh. I am sorry. I meant my other place."

He said, "You mean the nightclub called the Other Place?"

She replied, "No, I mean my other place on the lakefront. I have two apartments that I rent. One is on the South Side in Woodlawn, and the other one is on the North Side in Streeterville. Since that is so close to where we are, I thought it made sense to go there."

He was baffled, so he inquired: "Isn't that expensive? And how do you manage that on a nurse's salary?"

She smiled and paused before she spoke. She finally said, "I know that I told you that I worked in a hospital, but it is you who assumed that I was a nurse. I am a neurosurgeon at Northwestern Hospital that is not too far from here. I assure you I can manage to pay for both apartments."

He just said, "My apology."

Again, she smiled and quickly said: "No apology needed or required. I live in the recently completed Lake Point Tower complex near here. It's an architectural marvel inspired by Mies van der Rohe. You have heard of him, right?"

He hesitated but then said, "Yes. The Illinois Institute of Technology where he taught was just a little north of where I grew up as a young man. His reputation and the proximity of the college were partly responsible for my aspirations to attend college."

As they approached Lake Point Tower, she told him to go to Grand Avenue to get in the garage on the north side of the building. She also told him she would pay for valet parking for the evening. The parking garage was an underground, cavernous structure that was almost a city-block long. As the parking garage attendant opened the car for Karen to get out, he gently grabbed her left arm and told her, "Wait. I will help you get out of the car."

With that, he exited the car and handed the keys to the attendant, and told him he would help the lady out of the car. The attendant smiled and said, "Yes, sir." He then handed Gregory the ticket for parking the car. This time Gregory unabashedly looked at Karen's leg as she exited the car and gently grabbed her by the waist as soon as she was standing. Karen approved of that move and pecked him on the cheek.

She then said, "I live on the 32nd floor facing the lake. Tell me what you think of my place after you have seen it."

He replied, "I most certainly will do that. I am anxious to see what you have put together."

He had heard about the Mies van der Rohe-inspired building and was joyful at the opportunity to see it up close and what it looked like inside one of the apartments. He was not disappointed. Karen's apartment had views facing the lake and the north side of the city. Because the outer walls of the building (almost all glass) are curved, there is an aesthetics of the exterior façade and interior space that made Gregory gleeful. He had never seen or been in a building of this kind.

As a counterpoint to the curves of the apartment's interior, Karen had placed furniture in the apartment that was all rectangular except for a round dining room table. The base for almost all of the furniture was curved in one way or another to offer a counterpoint to the counterpoint. Gregory nodded his head several times to indicate to Karen that he approved of what she had done with her space. She acknowledged his approval by reaching out her hand and taking him straight to her bedroom.

Chapter Nine
How About Us

Gregory was ecstatic about having Karen as a companion and lover. He reveled in her beauty and intellect, and he fully immersed himself in their relationship, almost. In addition to seeing various jazz groups who visited the city, they enjoyed dinner at many of the best restaurants in the city. They also took advantage of the many outdoor activities available in the summer at various locations but especially along the lakefront.

Gregory did have two things that kept him from letting go and completely getting into Karen's world. The first thing was his sporadic but wonderful relationship with Sharon, which continued despite Karen and Sharon knowing about his relationship with both of them. The second thing was her work as a physician, which meant she had a lot of money to spend and was socially able to move in circles that he was comfortable in but sometimes uncomfortable.

Despite a bit of hesitancy about jumping feet first into Karen's world, this was a period in his life where most days could best be described as unbounded happiness. In addition to the joy he was able to bring to his life because of his loving relationships with Karen and Sharon, he delighted in his work as a teacher as he watched his students expand in their knowledge and wisdom of the world they inhabited.

His unbounded happiness abruptly ended on April 4, 1968, when he learned of Martin Luther King's brutal assassination in Memphis shortly after arriving home on that Thursday evening. He immediately thought about what he should do about going to school that following

Friday, but that decision came quickly as he thought about helping his students make some choices about responding to that dastardly deed.

He awoke early that Friday morning, turned on the television, and heard about the rioting that had started in various parts of the Black community in Chicago and various other cities. He wondered whether or not the students at his school would participate in the riot in Chicago. He realized that he would only know that directly if he went to the school.

He quickly showered, dressed, gulped down a glass of orange juice and a cup of coffee, rushed to his car, and drove as fast as he could to the school. In his mind, he has visions of the school going up in flames. But as he pulled into the staff parking lot on the south end of the school, he saw staff and students entering the main entrance to the school on what appeared to be a normal day.

The entire school was eerily quiet for the first three periods of the day, and at precisely 11:00 A.M., someone pulled the fire alarm. All of the students in the classroom quietly got up, walked out of class, and calmly walked upstairs from the second to the third floor. He followed his class to the third floor, where hundreds of students had gathered.

As if they had received a signal, all of the students started to run mindlessly in circles for two hours while staff and other students watched. The students did not utter a sound as they ran, and the only thing you could hear was a dull thunderous sound of feet on the concrete floor, which trembled like love's perfect symbol.

Again, as if on signal, at exactly 1:00 P.M., students stopped running and returned to their scheduled classes. The school returned to the eerily quiet state that it had been in before the running on the third floor had started. When the school day was over, students quietly left the building and went home.

He marveled at what had transpired that day, and he hoped that what had transpired was in part due to what he and his colleagues had imparted to students in so many different ways. He spent the weekend grieving over Dr. King's death, but he also embraced a resolve about continuing to help students understand and live Dr. King's ideas and ideals.

He got a call from both Karen and Sharon that Friday evening, but only Karen offered to get together for the evening. He assumed that Sharon's husband would be on duty, and she had decided to be at home with her children. He understood why Sharon would make the choice that she had made, but he secretly wished that she could have joined him and Karen at Karen's place in Streeterville.

As he pulled into the garage of Karen's building, he was still sad and down over the killing of Martin Luther King, but he hoped that Black folks would not destroy their own community and pursue other options for venting their frustration over the immediate precipitant for the riots and the many grievances that were more than four centuries old. As he rode the elevator to the 32nd floor of Lake Point Tower, he reflected on events in his life over the past several years.

A little more than two years ago, his father had passed. That thought brought tears to his eyes. When Karen opened the door to her apartment and saw him standing there with tears rolling down his cheeks; she immediately pulled him into the apartment and her breast. She said, "Do you want to talk about it?"

His reply was, "Yes."

His father died in a mental institution where he had been (off and on) for more than twenty years. The officials from the mental hospital told his family that he died of a heart attack.

When his family went to pick up his father's body to take it to the undertaker, one of the hospital orderlies said that it was rumored that his father had gotten into a fight with one of the other orderlies and had been beaten to death.

Gregory did not recall how that was resolved, but his father's death was never satisfactorily explained to his family. His father's wish was not to be buried in the cold, hard ground; and he had requested before his death to be cremated and have his ashes scattered to the winds off of Lake Michigan. Because of that wish, his remains were not available very long to pursue how he died.

He had always wondered about his father's origins and past. He had bits and pieces about his father's life. But he did not know a great deal about the man who had been in his life constantly at an early age and only episodically in his adolescent and early adulthood years. That was because of his father's frequent and extended stays in the Manteno State Hospital outside of Chicago.

He both knew at the time and after his father passed that state mental hospitals in the United States were not the best place for a man to be, especially a Black man. The issues of discrimination, gross neglect, mistreatment, rape, and even murder were constants in almost all such hospitals in the decades of the 30s thru the 60s (and beyond in some states).

However, the problem ran deeper than just a Black man trying to survive in the South in the late 19th and early 20th centuries. The problem involved miscegenation in America and efforts to establish cultural and legal boundaries between the rich and poor. That was a problem that existed from the moment Black people were first introduced into the American colonies as far back as 1619.

While the Great Migration mitigated for Blacks some of the social and economic problems that arose from just living in the South; before that, Blacks had moved around the states of the South (upper and lower) to try to escape the "one-drop rule" that almost everyone in the South would have been subjected to upon close examination.

From genealogy records, Gregory discovered that his father's family started out in South Carolina (on the border of Tennessee), left there and stayed in Memphis, Tennessee for a time, and ultimately wound up in Arkansas, where his father had been born.

In one census report, his grandmother on his father's side is described as white; in another as mulatto; and still another as Black. In various census records, she is also listed as being born in Mississippi, Arkansas, and Tennessee.

One of the explanations that Gregory was able to come up with was that his father's family had had a Small Migration before the

Great Migration to keep from being classified as slaves in the days before the Civil War.

As a result of the information Gregory found on the Internet, he was better able to understand some of the things he heard from his father and about his father. He knew then that his father did have siblings—three sisters and a brother. He knew then what his father meant when he talked about "some old White woman" being his mother.

He had occasionally heard about aunts on his father's side who lived in Mississippi or Tennessee or somewhere in the South. He vaguely remembered seeing a picture and hearing a name associated with one or both of those aunts. And it was even possible that at an early age, he had met Aunt Murdis and Aunt Drucilla. It was all kind of hazy and vague to him now.

As Gregory recalled, there had always been attempts to restrict Blacks in some way or another, and none of those restrictions ever worked, at least in the way that those imposing the restrictions wanted them to work. The movements of Blacks in America in general and in a variety of locales in America, in particular, were always problematic for both Blacks and for those who would keep them in their place, so to speak.

For the most part, that was problematic because of the various skin tones of Blacks. But early on, Blacks found ways to deal with restrictions and boundaries by living on the restrictions and boundaries (gravitas, if you will) rather than just within them. And living on the restrictions and boundaries didn't necessarily mean just physical mobility. It also meant psychological mobility that came with a certain style of being in the world.

For example, when Gregory's father left the family dwelling to go a few blocks over to the Stroll and dance the Jitterbug, Swing, Lindy hop, or some other dance that was popular at the time; or when Charlie Parker was finally able to play the tenor saxophone in a way that he could only initially feel; or when the Harlem Renaissance and Chicago Renaissance gave expression to a variety of emotions and feelings Blacks had about their circumstance and conditions related to living in America; all of those were attempts by a people to go beyond what was described and circumscribed for them by others who wanted them to only live in the gravitas of their earthly existence.

Music, dance, art, dress, speech, and other cultural expressions served to both transcend and allow enjoyment of life lived in a particular moment. Those same cultural expressions also served as a bond between people in a particular locale and time; but sooner or later, they would be found in geographically dispersed Black communities across America. The blues may have started in the Mississippi Delta, but it found local expressions as far away as Kansas, New Orleans, Chicago, and New York.

Karen listened carefully as Gregory talked about his father and other matters directly and indirectly related to his father and family, and she suddenly had another level of respect for him and the work he did as a teacher. She was almost a little jealous of him and the work that he did. She ordered dinner for them and opened another bottle of champagne. She then said, "So what are you going to do about Dr. King's death and the death of your father?"

He replied, "I have already committed to a life of teaching in the inner-city schools of Chicago, and I have thought about how I could live an exemplary life that is in keeping with the teachings of Dr. King."

Karen smiled and said: "I think you can easily do the first thing that you mentioned, but the second thing might be a little bit harder, depending upon how you define 'exemplary life.'"

He knew exactly what Karen meant, and he simply smiled and nodded his head at her comment. With that, he reached for the glass of champagne that had been poured for him. Then he said, "To the King."

Chapter Ten
The Examined Life

Gregory had learned early in life that accomplishing goals in life depended not just on what you were willing to do but also on what you were willing not to do. In other words, what you were willing to give up or stop doing. As he snuggled up with Karen after making love that evening, he started to think about what he would have to give up to live the exemplary life that he and Karen had talked about earlier.

The first thing that he thought about was the other relationship he had with Sharon. But he dismissed that as something he would have to give up because he was a single man and both ladies knew about and had agreed to their arrangement. There was a slight hitch in the arrangement because Sharon was still married and living with her husband and kids. However, that was mostly just a legal matter rather than an ethical one since Sharon and her husband were in divorce proceedings and living separate lives while remaining in the same house.

When he left Karen's house that following Sunday, he was suddenly in a funk as he headed to his condo. He was not sure what that was about. Given what had happened that prior week, his time with Karen was much beyond what he expected. So, he did not think that was the heart of his funk. Something else was gnawing at him.

As he entered the garage in his building, it occurred to him that while he was happy about having a relationship with two gorgeous women. What he wanted was a good, solid, exclusive relationship with one woman. He smiled at that thought but said to himself: *Yes!*

That's a significant part of my funk. I don't want to be switching back and forth between ladies. I want just one woman to hold, kiss, make love to, talk to, and run the streets with.

For the next several months, he just slid back from Karen and Sharon; and as he did so, he told them why. They both told him that they had already noticed and talked about his exit from their lives, and they, too, were ready for something different.

They also told Gregory that they were glad he did not try to choose one of them over the other. Karen had started to date a White physician from the hospital where she worked, and Sharon had decided to reconcile with her husband and move to Las Vegas.

By the time the school year had ended, Gregory had moved Karen and Sharon out of his orbit. In early June, they had gone to dinner together as sort of a farewell to love and friendship, and he had fervently fucked each one separately as a way of holding each of them in his mind and heart for as long as he could. No regrets from anyone involved, just a promise to stay in contact no matter who was in their life.

During the last week of school, he got two surprise invitations from organizations offering training and stipends for teachers in inner-city schools. Both were from universities located in Chicago. DePaul University offered a six-week summer program, "Law in American Society," obviously a response to the killing of Dr. King that prior spring.

The other invitation came from the University of Chicago and was a two-year program that would start that Fall after the regular school day. That program was a teacher-training program for new teachers and experienced teachers to improve their knowledge and skills for working in inner-city schools.

He quickly responded to both invitations and got accepted into both programs. The summer program started the week after school was out and was held at the downtown campus of DePaul University. The training was intense: five days a week for six hours a day. The group (sixty in number) was not as large as he had anticipated but still larger than he would have liked. On the first few days of training, he was laser-like focused on the words of the instructor, a law professor from DePaul's School of Law. By the end of the first week, however, he was acclimated enough to begin to look around to see who was in the course.

During the lunch break that Friday, he decided to sit with a group of Hyde Park High School teachers. The group was racially mixed, and a slightly rotund woman kept smiling at him without saying anything. Just as the group was leaving the dining area, he beckoned the woman to come over to him. As she reached the spot where he stood, he said: "I am Gregory Porter from DuSable High School. What's your name?"

She replied, "I am Julia Gruen. And you probably know that I am from Hyde Park High School."

He said, "How about having a drink with me after the session today."

She replied, "Okay. Where?"

His response was, "I am guessing that we both live in Hyde Park; how about the Jazzskeller in the Hyde Park Bank building?"

She said, "Or, since I live right around the corner from there, what if we just go to my place? I have several bottles of good German wine and a fabulous jazz collection."

His stomach tightened a little bit, but he said, "Sounds good. Give me your address."

He wasn't sure what Julia had in mind for the evening, but he thought he would check it out.

Her apartment was in a huge complex on 53rd Street and Harper Avenue. Her unit was a nicely appointed three-bedroom affair with huge bay windows that allowed the sun to flood the apartment with light, making it feel good to be in that space. He thought to himself: *I could live here.*

Julia brought him a glass of Blue Nun; a decent but relatively inexpensive wine imported from Germany. Since he preferred wines that were sort of sweet, he thought her taste in wine came close to a perfect match to his. As he took his first sip from the large goblet, he heard the opening strings to a tune by Charlie Parker called "Laura." He had always liked that tune by Parker. "April in Paris" was the next tune to play. He took another sip of the wine, and his mind went back to the time he was in Paris while stationed in Germany.

Whenever he thought about Paris, he thought of beautiful ladies, romance, sex, jazz, and walks along the Champs-Élysées during the summer when the breeze would blow the dresses of the ladies high enough to get flashes of thighs up and down the street. As the next tune started, "I'm In The Mood for Love," he was brought back to reality by the touch of Julia pulling him up to dance with her on that number. He pushed himself into her ample breast, held her gently with both arms, and moved gracefully to the beautiful sounds of Bird's playing and the graceful notes of the strings behind him.

When that song ended, Julia took his hand and led him into her bedroom. That was a surprise, and he was tempted to resist. Instead, he watched her disrobe and put on full display her Rubenesque and visually stimulating body. She then undressed him. They never said a word after they were disrobed. They simply held each other gently, kissed wherever either was inclined to kiss, and floated into a heavenly state that went on for several hours.

He woke to the sound of an up-tempo tune by Parker called "In The Still Of The Night." He had always liked that number because of the chorus that accompanied Parker's playing. The chorus went as fast and as high as Parker; and whenever he listened to the tune, he always thought of himself as being able to sing as fast and as high as Parker and the chorus. Of course, that was not possible, but it was fun thinking about it.

He and Julia spent the summer working in the course they were enrolled in. Each day after the class ended and on weekends; they would take a stroll in nearby Grant Park along Michigan Avenue or one of the other parks in the city, check out an exhibit at one of the many museums in the city, walk the many trails on the lakefront, see a play or jazz performance, have dinner at one of the many world-class restaurants in the city, check out a baseball game being played by the Sox or Cubs, or take their lovemaking to another level in the bed of one or the other.

It was, indeed, one of the best summers of his life, and he wondered how he could keep the music playing. He couldn't. After school started in the Fall; he and Julia often talked by phone, but his and her schedule did not permit them to see much of one another.

Then one Saturday afternoon, while shopping in the Hyde Park Coop grocery store, he saw Julia talking to and holding hands with a White dude. He was not close enough to speak to her without shouting, so he simply smiled and waved. She did the same. They seldom talked to or saw each other after that day.

He missed Julia. She was fun to be around. She was one of the brightest women he had ever known, and she could engage him in conversations about a wide range of topics that often stretched him intellectually. She also cooked well, and her taste in clothes was perfect. On top of all of that, the sex with her was magical in some ways.

He had known from the beginning, however, that there were boundaries around their relationship, mostly having to do with ethnicity. Julia was from a wealthy Jewish family in New York City; Gregory was from a poor African-American family in Chicago. For a few months, they continued to occasionally talk on the phone. By the time the Fall had ended, that even stopped.

That was okay because he did not have a lot of time to think about Julia or any ladies at that point. He had been given advanced placement courses to teach that Fall, which required a lot of preparation to stay on top of his classes. In addition, the training program at the University of Chicago had started, which also took up a lot of his time after school. He didn't know what to expect in terms of actual content or activities for the program, but he liked the concept around which the program was designed.

From his own experience, he knew that educators in their various school roles (teacher, administrator, counselor, etc.) were trained, worked, and pretty much thought of themselves in isolation from one another. This program was designed to help educators in their various roles to prepare, work, and think about themselves as a social system whose ability to maximize students' learning depended upon how well that social system functioned. Conceptually and theoretically, that made so much sense; he just embraced the program because of its sheer aesthetics.

In the Fall of 1968, he decided to enroll in a course and apply for a doctorate. He had some trepidation about those moves because he knew the demands already being made on his time. He felt, however, that might be a good thing because it would take his mind off of Karen, Sharon, and Julia. It did, but it did not turn out to be nearly as stressful as he thought it would be. Intellectually it was the most invigorating period of his life.

Socially, too, his life was on fire. He continued to party with the staff of the high school on many occasions. Then he started to get invitations from various groups and individuals at the university to attend academically-oriented affairs and social gatherings all over Chicago. Despite the demands from his job, the courses he was taking, and his social life; he flourished and often felt euphoric as he responded to all the things he had to contend with daily. There were days and weeks when he felt that this must be heaven.

His buddy and mentor at the school saw him in the hall one Friday afternoon and practically begged him to come to his lady's house for dinner and cocktails. His buddy also added that his lady friend had a friend that wanted to meet him. He was intrigued by that idea, so he agreed to join him after school. He was more than happy to join his buddy and mentor that evening, and he thought about how he first met Eddie.

In his first year of teaching in the upper grades of the high school, he had been assigned to lunchroom duty during the same period as Eddie. On the very first day of lunchroom duty, Eddie, a tall and heavy-set man, welcomed him and offered to show him the ropes of supervising the students at lunch. The first thing he told him was to always move about the lunchroom so that he would have a full view of the room. He also told him to keep his back to the wall. Gregory laughed at that because it made him think of the cowboy movies and saying in the streets of Chicago: Never sit with your back to the door!

Eddie was a teacher in the social studies department and wanted to be his friend for some reason. During the first semester of teaching in the upper grades, he would often meet Eddie at Bernard's, a joint on 71st and Vernon right off of South Parkway. He was never sure why he was so comfortable in that place and with the crowd there, but he would spend hours after school guzzling Budweiser beer, shooting pool in a backroom, and talking smack with Eddie and men who just seemed to want to waste away the hours of their life.

After a few months of doing that, he had decided to return to school and get his master's. Eddie had long before received his master's and continued to hang in Bernard's until he met a pretty woman named Lorice, who joined the staff of DuSable late in the school year as a home economics teacher. Eddie was smitten, and that summer, Eddie and Lorice became an item. If you saw Lorice, you saw Eddie; and if you saw Eddie, you saw Lorice. They did make a handsome couple, and you could tell that they were really into each other.

When he got to Lorice's house on 71st Street and East End Avenue (just east of Stoney Island Avenue), he was surprised to see Sharon sitting at a table with a glass of champagne in her hand. Lorice and Eddie both broke out in a hearty laugh, and they were joined by him and Sharon. He was comfortable in that moment in that situation, and Sharon appeared to be the same. They spoke, and then they embraced, perhaps longer than either intended. It was like returning home after a long, long trip.

Both Lorice and Eddie were good cooks, so what they prepared for the evening was delicious. They had Cornish hens and dressing, sautéed fresh string beans and onions, boiled fresh corn on the cob, and baked deep-dish peach cobbler. As he sat and talked and ate and drank with his friends, Gregory quietly exhaled. He was home. Really home!

The four of them were having such a great time that they had not noticed the heavy snow that had fallen that evening. By the time

Gregory looked out the window, eighteen inches of snow had fallen and continued to come down at a rate so heavy that he could not see the buildings on the next block and could barely see the streetlights. He called them all to the window to witness what they all talked about and thought might be a repeat of the blizzard of the previous year.

Lorice said, "It does not make sense for you all to try to get home tonight. Eddie and I can sleep in my room. Why don't the two of you take the bed in my other room?"

Sharon hesitated to speak, but Gregory quickly said, "Yes. I would like that. And Sharon, I will not try to do anything funny. Unless you want me to or tell me to."

Everyone laughed, and Sharon said, "We shall see."

Chapter Eleven
It's Complicated

Gregory did try something funny that evening as he and Sharon got into bed together, but it was something that Sharon told him she wanted and had been thinking about for a long time since the last time they had been together. After their lovemaking had ended that evening, Sharon told him how she had gone to Vegas to try to get her life back together with her husband and children. She told him that had not worked because her husband continued to run the streets and spend only a little time with her and the kids. She said that she had no regrets, but she was done with that marriage.

Gregory was both happy and alarmed at the same time to hear those words. He had thought about Sharon and Karen often after they left one another's bed, but he had been free to run the streets for a while now, and he wasn't sure he wanted to be in an exclusive relationship again with anyone, especially after the brief affair with Julia. That breakup did hurt a little more than he thought it would, and it certainly hurt a lot more than he would have admitted to anyone other than himself. He decided that he did not have to worry for the moment because Sharon was still married. So, he kissed her right breast and lips and turned over, and then he fell asleep without saying a word.

The next morning, they all realized that the snowfall had not been as bad as the blizzard of the prior year, but it was still heavy enough to keep them snowbound for a few days. Lorice told them not to worry. She had enough food and liquor to last two weeks. They heard on the television and radio that Chicago Public Schools would be closed for the week and possibly longer to clear the streets and make it safe for staff and students to get to school.

Lorice fixed a simple but delicious breakfast that morning, and everyone settled in for what they knew would be a few days, at minimum, together in a confined but elegant space. That afternoon they played bid whist for a few hours, although Lorice was not very good at the game. Sharon was good at playing the game, and even Eddie conceded that.

They switched partners with Lorice and Gregory now playing against a dynamo pair, Sharon and Eddie, to even things up a bit. Surprisingly, Lorice and Gregory won almost as many games as Sharon and Eddie. Gregory thought that his calm demeanor helped Lorice be less intimidated by others at the table. Unlike Eddie, he never criticized Lorice when she made a mistake.

Later that afternoon, Sharon and Gregory said they wanted to take a nap, but they wanted to make love again. Both Lorice and Eddie smiled at that bit of deception and started playing a card game that two could play. Sharon and Gregory knew each other's body well, so they were able to make love tenderly without a lot of commotion. In the early evening, they emerged from the bedroom fully dressed and looking well-rested.

Lorice and Eddie had already cooked and were waiting for their companions to join them for dinner. This time Sharon and Gregory said they wanted to serve dinner. No one objected, and the two got busy acting as if they were the hosts for the evening. The actual hosts had prepared mixed greens (mustard and turnip) with smoked turkey, dressing, candied sweet potatoes, deep-fried catfish, and a deep-dish apple pie. When he saw what had been prepared for dinner, Gregory smiled and kissed Lorice and Eddie on the cheek. Eddie vigorously wiped that side of his face with his hand, and everyone chuckled.

The snow was cleared from the streets of Chicago quicker than anyone anticipated. By Wednesday of the following week, schools and offices were open, and everyone had returned to their normal routine for that time of year. Before they saw each other at Lorice's place, Gregory did not know that Sharon had returned to Chicago after only a few months in Vegas, and she had taken a job as an assistant principal at a school on the near north side of Chicago. That was interesting because he had turned down a job as an assistant principal at the same school that year. He wanted to stay at DuSable on the South Side.

The second quarter had already started at the university, and with Sharon sort of back in his life, things got complicated. In a class he had taken in the first quarter of the school year, he met a cute young Black girl from Milwaukee, Wisconsin. They never talked about dating exclusively or anything like that, but they jumped right into a sexual thing after she had invited him to come over for dinner and had sex with him before she had even prepared the meal. She explained to him that she already had a close boyfriend at another university in the city, and she was still seeing a male friend who still lived and worked in Milwaukee: A sort of fuck buddy that she still liked a lot.

He always had fun and enjoyed himself when he was with Jazmin. He could always be himself and talk about anything. Their relationship was always about the moment— never the past or the future. Neither he nor Jazmin had a lot of time to be together. The demands on his time were greater than on her time, but she still had a lot to do because she was carrying a full load of classes each quarter. He had only one course to take each quarter, although he worked full time and participated in the teacher training program at the university.

And then things got even more complicated when he started a course in the second quarter. This was an exhilarating class taught by a professor who would become his favorite professor at the university. What made it even more enjoyable was the attention he got from a White girl in the class who decided to make him a study buddy.

Jeanette initially kept things on the straight up. But one evening, while they were studying in the Regenstein Library, she asked him to take her to the stacks in a remote part of the library to find a book she needed. There she pulled up her dress, removed her panties, told him to keep it quiet, unzipped his pants, and gently pulled him into her. They both had to cover the mouth of the other so that they would not be discovered doing something that was against the rules of the library, although neither had seen that posted anywhere.

When they finished, they straightened their attire and returned to the desk where they had been studying. On the way back, Jeanette randomly grabbed a book off the shelf and brought it back to the table as if that was something she intended to use. Interestingly, they continued to study for a midterm exam that would take place in a few days, and they could concentrate on that despite the antics they had just engaged in.

As they left the library, she offered to buy dinner at a local pizzeria located a few blocks east of the library. Gregory told her, "I don't have a lot of spare time, but I am hungry. And I do need to eat."

She said, "I just wanted to be with you a little bit longer. That was fun, but I like just being in your company."

He replied, "And I like being in your company. Was what we did in the library something you had planned?"

She replied, "No, not exactly. I have wanted to make love to you for a while now, but I never thought of doing that in the library until tonight. It was enjoyable, but it certainly would have been a lot more comfortable in my bed or your bed."

He smiled at that and said, "Yes. Next time let's try your bed or mine."

She laughed and said, "Maybe!"

He did not see or hear from Jeanette for several weeks until he got a call from her asking him to come to her apartment for dinner. Her place was not too far from the main quadrangle and just east of 57th and Woodlawn. Her place reminded him of a place that he had only imagined seeing because it was something that he thought of as being out in the woods somewhere. Yet, it was a comforting environment with a lot of wood furniture. I guess the best word to describe her apartment would be "rustic."

She had finished cooking and asked, "Are you ready to eat? His reply was, "Yes. I am starving."

Jeanette had prepared a simple meal: fried fish, French fries, sautéed string beans, and a Dutch cookie of some kind. When they got to the end of the meal and were eating the cookie, that's when she told him she was Dutch and from a small village not far from Amsterdam. He smiled as she talked about her origins, and he thought about how he and a buddy had driven to Amsterdam when he was in the service in Germany.

Back then, Gregory had just bought a used Mercedes-Benz from a fellow who was rotating back to the States, and he got it dirt cheap. Amsterdam was not far from where they were stationed, Karlsruhe, a small town in the western part of Germany on the French-German border and Rhone-Rhine river. The drive was a little less than three hundred and fifty miles northwest of the army installation.

As they traveled across the no-speed-limit autobahn, he and Pat talked about how that bit of modern technology had probably facilitated Germany's swift conquest of most of Western Europe during World War II. They also talked about the fact that, in reality, all of Western Europe was not much bigger than the United States, and they both wondered how a nation as small as Germany could initiate a conflagration that ended up with almost the entire world being involved and consumed by its flames.

Pat, his service buddy, had been to Amsterdam several times before they went together; and at one time, Pat had considered marrying a young lady that he had met there. Pat told him how the family had welcomed him, and he had even been able to stay in the young lady's home, sleep in the same bed with her there, and make love to her while the parents were at home while they did so. Gregory thought that was strange and interesting, but it was in keeping with what little he knew about the Dutch people.

He started to talk to Jeanette about his time in Germany and visit to Amsterdam, but he decided that could wait for another time. That decision was reinforced when Jeanette put on the LP by Miles Davis called "My Funny Valentine." It wasn't until after they had made love that he realized that the tempo of their lovemaking had closely paralleled that of the music on the LP, even the up-tempo "All Blues."

Jeanette asked that he stay the night, but that was something he did not like doing.

He rarely spent the night at any woman's house, and he seldom allowed women to spend the night at his place. So, he made some lame excuse about why he had to leave, and he just said to Jeanette, "I will call you next week."

As he drove home, he thought to himself, *Damn, that was a hard fuck*. He had never thought about making love in those terms; but over the years, he would come to categorize or place his sexual encounters on a continuum from "soft fuck" to "hard fuck."

Before he had the opportunity to call Jeanette that following week, she had called him and asked him to meet her at Jimmy's, a campus hangout for students and Hyde Park locals who were comfortable with being in the same environment as students from the university.

Jimmy's was an exciting place because it was where you could see a good cross-section of the Hyde Park community: students, construction workers, professors, theologians, Blacks, Whites, Jews, Middle Easterners, gays, lesbians, poor, rich, and middle class.

They served food at Jimmy's, so he had a cheeseburger, fries, and a beer. Jeanette had the same, and she requested that they do the Heineken beer thing in a salute to her homeland. He was good with that, although he usually drank Budweiser. Early in the evening, Jeanette's conversation was about little or nothing. But then she said, "I am going to be finished with my PhD work in another year and a half."

He thought that was odd because she had only been there for two years. Most students spent eight years or more getting a doctorate. He said to her, "How did you manage that? It usually takes several years to finish the coursework and several more to find a dissertation topic and complete the dissertation process."

Jeanette said, "Well, first you have to brownnose all of your professors, and then you have to find one professor who wants to get in your draws in a bad way. Then you wait until there is an opportunity to have a late appointment in his office; lock his office door as soon as you walk in, and then you just raise your dress to show him that you have on no panties; then you fuck his brains out!"

They both laughed at that last comment, and he said: "Well, I am not sure how that would work for me."

She replied, "Trust me. It could, and I don't mean you have to do that in terms of a male instructor." She winked after that comment.

He went home with Jeanette that night and many nights after that. When summer arrived, they would often go to the 63rd Street Beach and the Promontory to just sit and talk or not talk. On one of those evenings at the Promontory, she decided to tell him that that was one of her favorite places to visit during the summer. She also told him that was where she would often pick up men and have sex with them wherever they could: in a car, hotel room, her place, his place, in the bushes, and sometimes in a classroom on campus.

He had had an inkling that Jeanette was kind of freaky, but he had not anticipated what she finally told him that evening: That she had once been a nun but found that not even that environment could tame her hypersexuality, so they had cast her out of the nunnery like the devil had been cast from heaven. He thought to himself, *What have I done? We have had protected sex most of the time, but there have been a few occasions where we didn't use protection. Fuck!*

Chapter Twelve
I Could Have Loved You

He was never again intimate with Jeanette, although they occasionally talked on the phone or visited for a minute when they bumped into one another on campus. He had this sense that Jeanette wanted more from him than he was ever going to be able to give; and, indeed, he wanted more from her than he thought she would ever be able to give him.

He had figured out over time that that is why most relationships end: one or both parties in the relationship want more than the other can give. There is usually a wide range of things one person or the other wants or needs: Time, money, sex, attention, intellectual stimulation, conversation, a willingness to go places, and so on. And there is a wide range of reasons one person or the other puts forth as to why they are not able to give the other person what they want or need. Often, the reasons for not giving are bogus, but sometimes they run deep into the other person's core and how they want to be in the world.

After the affair with Jeanette, he decided he would take a hiatus from dating and the stuff that usually accompanied that. It was not a decision made entirely concerning what went down with Jeanette. He was stressed-out from all of the demands being made on him, and he just needed time to be alone with himself. He routinely returned to his condo each day after work and whatever other activities that he had to engage in that day. And on the weekends, he spent longer periods sleeping than he had ever done.

After a few months of that, he was sufficiently rested and bored enough to get back out into the world. He was still not ready to run the streets with a companion, so he bought single tickets to various events that featured people or groups that brought him joy. One of those events featured the Alvin Ailey American Dance Theater. He had seen the group several times before but never alone. He had decided to take a cab from his condo because he knew that would be more convenient and cheaper.

As he stepped from the cab in front of the theater, a tall attractive woman emerged from the parking lot behind him. She immediately got his attention because she did not move from where she stood even though there was little traffic in the street. He recognized that she was afraid to move because where they stood was not a place to safely cross six lanes of traffic to reach the entrance to the theater. He gently took her hand and held it to help her safely move across the street.

He said, "Do you have a ticket yet?"

She replied, "Yes, I have a ticket."

He needed to get his ticket from will call, so he said, "If you can wait a minute until I get my ticket, I would like to buy you a drink."

She said, "Okay."

An Alvin Ailey show in Chicago is a big deal. And as he stepped into the entrance to the Auditorium Theater with his new companion at his side, he was happy to see so many people of various hues and ethnicities mingling and having fun at a point before they had even seen the show.

They only had about thirty-five minutes before the show started; but he decided to get her a drink, find out her name, determine if she would be sitting anywhere near him, see if he could get a number for future contact, and perhaps even ask her to join him in a conversation over dinner after the show. Twenty-five minutes before the start of the show, he had done all of that.

He got her (and him) a glass of champagne, found out her name was Alice, learned that she would be sitting not too far from him, got her business card (to which she added the number for her home phone), and was gleeful about her agreement to go to dinner with him after the show. They chatted for a bit longer and, with drinks in hand, headed for their respective seats. He stood and watched Alice walk away from him and thought to himself: *The gods are looking down upon me.*

Alice was inclined to talk a little more than he liked, but she was a gorgeous woman. Even with heels, she was still a little shorter than him, which he liked. She had a fabulous shape that rivaled many of the movie stars of the day, and she had a face prettier than most movie stars of the day. As he sat and watched the opening numbers of the performance, he was swept up in the movements and music of that moment. John Coltrane's "Dear Lord" was the first piece heard on the show, and he wondered how could a human being create such heavenly music. He was near to tears as the dancers crawled, flew, jumped, and gracefully embraced one another to convey whatever the music was saying at one point or another.

The rest of the evening was a variation on the beauty and grace of the opening piece of the performance. He thought about Alice and how she might be feeling about what they both were witnesses to in different parts of the theater. Then it was over. He rushed to the spot in the entrance to the auditorium to see if he could find her there.

As he approached the bar where they had bought drinks and stood and talked, she stood there smiling and waving at him to make sure he saw her. She was enchanting, and he thought to himself: *I could love this woman.*

Since she had parked across the street from the Auditorium Theater and he had taken a cab, they thought it would be best if they just walked to a small restaurant around the corner on Michigan Avenue to have dinner. She took his left hand and thanked him for helping her across Congress Boulevard, buying her a drink, and being such a gentleman. He smiled at that, but he felt it should have been him that thanked her for allowing him to be with her for the evening. However, neither spoke again after she expressed thanks until they were in the small restaurant seated next to one another.

He said to her, "How did you like the show?"

She replied, "I loved it. I have seen the dance company many times before, but this was the one I enjoyed the most. They brought me into the performance the moment the music from the opening dance started. 'Dear Lord,' by Coltrane is such a marvelous piece. What about you? Did you like the show?"

He told her that he agreed with her: That this performance was one he liked the most of the several performances he had seen by the company.

She looked down at his left hand and said, "I see you are not married. How could that be?"

He replied, "I often wonder about that myself. But I could raise the same question about you probably for the same reasons."

They both laughed in unison at that remark, but neither tried to answer the question that had been asked directly and indirectly. He suspected that the truth of the matter was that they both had suitors in their life but had not been inclined to enter into a relationship that led to marriage. As they continued to talk, he could not help but stare at this beautiful Black woman sitting near him. He decided at that moment that, at minimum, he would court her and see where he could take a relationship with her.

The next time that they met was at a party given by a mutual friend. They had not talked about meeting or being at the party together. Yet, once they were in the same setting, they did act as if they were an item: holding hands, dancing together during back-to-back records, talking and laughing heartily together, and staring at each other as if they had not met before.

He said to her, "Let's head up north to Rush Street for dinner. I am hungry."

They wound up at a nice little Italian restaurant not too far from Faces, a disco in the Rush Street area. He was giddy as he sat and talked to Alice and enjoyed a simple scampi and spaghetti dish. She had a stuffed trout dish that made him think that perhaps he should have gotten the same. They must have been thinking the same thing at the moment because each stuck a fork into the plate of the other as if they had rehearsed. They both nodded in some kind of agreement about how tasty the food was from the other's plate.

For the whole evening, he had watched her move her prodigious body without saying a word about what was evoked in him by the watching. But as they walked down Rush Street to the place where they had parked the car, he told her: "I want to go home with you tonight."

She turned to him, took his hand, and said: "I know."

She lived in a high-rise in South Commons, an area not too far from where he lived in Hyde Park. South Commons had been part of federal, state, and local authorities' efforts to provide subsidized housing on the south and west sides of Chicago other than the housing projects provided by the Chicago Housing Authority. Her apartment was not a luxurious place, but it was a lovely space that was nicely decorated.

She offered him a drink, but she only had wine as an option. He didn't care because that was not what he desired. He wanted her. She teased him a bit by quickly going to the bedroom and putting on a see-through gown that left only a little to the imagination. He decided to tease her, too, by slowly sipping the wine and just talking with her with all of his clothes on, including his suit coat and shoes. He saw her getting a little irritated, and he slowly slipped off his shoes, jacket, pants, socks, and underwear. He then sat in the oversize chair and said to her: "I am ready."

She smiled and said, "You are just fucking with me, right?"

He replied, "Just a little bit."

As she walked towards him, she decided to take off the see-through gown that she had on to allow him to have an unfettered view of her body. He almost came at that moment without her even touching him.

She saw him squirm and squirt a little, and she said to him: "Now, I just want to fuck with you a little bit."

Instead of joining him on the chair where he sat, she walked away from him and into the bedroom. He had not expected that move but immediately followed her into the bedroom. As he stepped into her bedroom, he had thoughts about immediately jumping her bones; but as soon as he had one foot in the room, he became motionless.

Three of the four walls in Alice's bedroom had one or two prints of paintings by Lawrence Jacobs and Romare Bearden. These were two of his all-time favorite artists, and he became so engrossed in looking at those paintings that he almost forgot about Alice, who was in the bed on her back with her legs wide open and one leg bent and cocked to the right. What a sight—the paintings in the background and Alice with her seductive position grinning at him.

His body jerked for a second, and he moved slowly to get close to Alice because he did not want her to think that he was too anxious to get next to her awe-inspiring body. Since she had offered up her body as if asking for oral sex, that is what he gave her for the first fifteen minutes or so of their lovemaking—in the exact position that he first saw her when he entered the bedroom. He then had her move her body down so that he could easily enter her, and then he took them both to some remote corner of the universe.

Chapter Thirteen
Surprise

Despite him being busy, he and Alice continued to see one another over the next several years. Both knew that it would end one day because she wanted to get married and have a kid or two. He was not inclined to want to embrace either of those states of being. Still, they always enjoyed one another's company, but she occasionally would tell him how hard it was to stay with him because she wanted to be married and have a child or two or three.

When she told him one day that she was pregnant and wanted to have an abortion, he was somewhat surprised but not really. As she explained to him, "You are not inclined to be married or have a child, so I don't want to put that kind of pressure on you. I would like for you to take me to the clinic and pay for the procedure if that is not a problem for you."

His initial thought to himself about the matter was, *But I thought you were taking birth control pills.*

But he knew that this was not the time to discuss that, and he quietly said, "Yes, I will take you to the clinic, and I will pay for the abortion. Are you sure that this is what you want?"

She replied, "Yes, this is what I want—for you and me."

On Wednesday of the following week, they went to an abortion clinic on the South Side in the Hyde Park neighborhood. They had been told that the staff of the clinic came from the two of the best schools of medicine in the world, although those schools were not named, and the doctors were only identified by their last name. The procedure took only a few hours, and they went to his condo in Hyde Park afterward for her to rest and get some food.

Alice did not talk to Gregory about the abortion that evening or ever. He never knew whether she had chosen a chemical or surgical procedure, what the gender of the child was or if she even knew, how far along her pregnancy had been (except it was within the first trimester), whether it was in any way painful, or her thoughts and feelings about choosing to have an abortion. He did sense that she never forgave him for allowing her to have an abortion, and not too long afterward, she told him that she had met another fellow closer to her in age and that she wanted to pursue that relationship.

He wished her luck and love and cried himself to sleep that night. He willed himself not to call her for several weeks after she told him about the other fellow. In the late evening on Wednesday of the fourth week, after he had last spoken to Alice, he got a phone call from her. She said softly, "You just trying to fuck with me?"

He replied, "I don't understand. You were the one to break it off with me."

She said, "I did not. I just told you I wanted to pursue another relationship. I didn't tell you I didn't want to see you anymore."

He chuckled and said kindly, "So you want to have your cake and eat it too?"

She said, "What's funny about that?"

He said, "To you, perhaps it isn't. To me, it sounds like you want to play a game that you have neither told me about nor given me the rules to play."

She said, "I want you to come and get me and take me to your place for the night."

He said, "Okay. See you in about a half-hour."

He picked her up from her Aunt's house where she stayed and drove back to his place.

As they rode the elevator to the 19th floor, she leaned against him and said: "So is this your last fuck with me?"

He said, "Yes."

He thought to himself: *And that's the way every man-woman relationship should end: One last good fuck*!

She stepped away from him and then off the elevator. She apparently had not expected that response from him because she started to softly cry as he opened the door to his condo. Seeing her cry at that moment made him tearful.

He had not been aware of the degree to which he loved Alice, and the pain of losing her was almost too much to endure. Had he been younger (or perhaps older), he would have settled down with Alice and had a few kids;

but that was not what he wanted or needed at that moment in his life.

Indeed, Sharon had said to him several times over the years that she wanted him to marry her and that she already had kids and that should make that an easier decision than the one involving Alice. And it was. Alice left his bed and condo that next morning. He only saw her once after that at a bus stop on 55th Street and Hyde Park Boulevard. Although he only had a short conversation with her; as he gazed at a pretty round face and shiny shoulder-length hair, he did think, *She may be the one who got away*!

Almost three years after they had gotten back into each other's life, Sharon and Gregory were married in a small ceremony in a small church on the South Side of Chicago with just some of his family members and her children in attendance. They were good together most of the time, but she wanted more than he could give.

Initially, they did not even inhabit the same space. Gregory was in his condo, and Sharon remained in her marital abode with her two children, both of whom had now reached their majority. They did party together and took trips abroad to Spain and other places on the European continent. But after one trip to the Sun Coast of Spain (Torremolinos), she had asked that he allow her and her daughter to move into his place to live. He had always thought of his condo as a private sanctuary, so he told her that was not possible.

That was a turning point in their relationship because she felt his response was a rejection of her and her daughter. Of course, it was not a rejection of her or her daughter. It was more a rejection of a particular way of living that she had proposed. He felt that if she wanted them all to be under one roof, she should have talked about how that could happen in a new space that they could jointly choose and purchase.

Gregory and Sharon continued to see one another for several years, although they lived in separate places. Their time running the streets together and lovemaking continued to be great, but both became less frequent at some point. They both had noticed that, and they decided one evening to talk about that over dinner. She told him that she loved him, but she was tired of the arrangement that they both had agreed to. She told him that she had met a gentleman who at least wanted to share a bed and live in the same space with her. So, she asked him for a divorce.

He had seen that coming, so he said, "Can we still be in each other's life as friends?"

She wryly smiled and said, "I don't want to be your damn friend."

Chapter Fourteen
Make Me Your Future

He sat at his desk that summery Sunday evening and took in an incredible view of Chicago's skyline from almost all imaginable viewpoints: West, North, East, and South (a small bit of it at least). That past week and weekend had been one of the strangest periods in his entire life: He had lost huge amounts of money in the stock market that Friday. That Saturday, he received a certified letter from a company he worked for (as a part-time writer and consultant) telling him that they no longer needed his service. Several months before that, his wife of four years suddenly walked out of his life. And earlier that day, the Chicago White Sox lost a game by one point to a team that they were to have handily beat.

He had no idea of how to process what had happened over the past weeks and months, and he absolutely could not make sense of any of it. At that moment of his life, he thought about going to the balcony of his apartment and plunging nineteen floors down to his death.

The only thing that stopped him from doing that was the thought of his two daughters. One of his daughters was actually Sharon's daughter, so she was technically a stepdaughter. The other daughter was born out-of-wedlock to an older woman he had a brief affair with and got pregnant. Because of her age, she decided she did not want an abortion or marriage with Gregory.

Sharon's daughter was in her third year of college and doing well. His other daughter was in the process of starting divorce proceedings from her husband of twelve years. His thought was that he had to help both daughters to finish a critical phase in their life.

Instead of leaping to his death; he shaved, showered, dressed, and headed out the door to a jazz joint not too far from where he lived. The place was fairly crowded for a late Sunday night show. He thought to himself: *These are the people who really want to live.* He took a seat in the reserved section of the room and ordered a bottle of champagne. After the waitress served him a glass of champagne, she inquired: "What are you celebrating or toasting?"

He coyly smiled and said, "Life."

The waitress subtlety nodded her head and smiled. She then said, "Yes, yes."

He watched the waitress walk away and thought to himself, *Cute!*

He settled back into his seat and waited for Roy Hargrove to take the stage with his group. For his last show in Chicago for the year, Hargrove had added a well-known local musician named Corey Wilkes, who also played trumpet. A year later, Hargrove would be gone: Dead from a heart attack and kidney failure.

But that evening, he and his young protégé gave one of those stellar performances that you remember for a very long time. And as he sat and listened to all of the music that made his heart sing that evening, he was happy that he had not jumped off the balcony of his apartment.

He had heard on the streets that the woman who had walked out of his life several months ago was said to be dating a fellow who was a friend of her first husband. He was kind of a decent fellow; but because he was a known womanizer, few people trusted him, not even the women he bedded.

He thought about getting back into Sharon's life, but he decided against that. So, for the fourth time in his life, he decided to get his player's card back out and activated. That was not a hard choice to make. He worked as a teacher full-time and was enrolled in a doctoral program at The University of Chicago and knew he would not have a lot of time to be in the streets.

He had heard a lot about his ex-wife, Sharon, through the grapevine, but he did not see her after their last supper and last fuck some months ago. He was sad about that, but he did not have time to think about her or any serious relationship. Almost all of his waking hours was consumed by work on his jobs and his courses.

At the end of two years of arduous work and studying, he was able to finally raise his head and look around at other things going around him. So, on a Friday near the end of the school year, he decided to hang with a group of staff members who had decided to go to the President's Lounge on 75th Street between ML King Drive and Cottage Grove Avenue. That Friday was the last day of the second week in

June when school would end for that academic year.

The lounge was crowded, but he could see an attractive woman sitting at the bar with her legs crossed and a martini in hand. She must have noticed him because she glanced at him and smiled and turned away. He looked carefully at her and saw that she had on a short black leather skirt with black stockings attached to a garter belt that allowed a bit of skin to show between the top of the stockings and the apparatus that held the garter belt.

He hesitated and then sat next to her at the bar. He immediately introduced himself and offered to buy her a drink. She accepted his offer and leaned into him and said, "You like what you see?"

He replied, "Yes, a lot."

They both laughed heartily at that exchange. Gregory's next move was to ask her to Bop on a song by Carl Carlton called "She's A

Bad Mama Jama (She's Built, She's Stacked)."
She could dance well, and the record aptly
described her physically and the way she
moved on the dance floor:

Poetry in motion.

He asked her name and told her his name.
He continued to hold her hand after the song
ended and pulled her back to the dance floor
when the DJ dropped "Joy and Pain" by Frankie
Beverly and Maze on the turntable. Stella was
so smooth and sensuous in those moments that
his stare could have burned a hole through
her. And when the "Sweetest Taboo" by Sade
came on, he almost lost his mind watching her
body respond to the sensuous sound of Sade.

After the last song; they sat for a minute,
chatted about much of nothing, rubbed one
another's leg, and stared and smiled at each
other. Then "Lady" by The Whispers started
to play. They both gently reached for the
other's hand and moved to the dance floor.

They were only one minute into the record before he said to her, "Let me take you home with me tonight."

Her reply was simply, "Give me a moment to think about that." Then they both pulled each other closer and went into a zone that Gregory was sure would end in intimacy later that evening.

She finally said to him, "Can we take this a bit slower? I am charmed by you, but I get the feeling that you are more of a player than someone interested in a serious relationship."

He replied, "You are almost right, but I am not interested in a one-night stand. Neither am I a dude who likes to kiss and tell. I am interested in finding a woman who is going my way, and that determines whether or not I enter into a serious relationship."

Stella replied, "I like that response, although I am sure that I do not fully understand all of what you were trying to say in that comment.

I am interested in finding out more about what you meant, so let's just hang together a little longer tonight and make a date to see one another again soon. Does that sound good?"

With that, she reached between his legs and rubbed his inner thigh, nibbled his ear, and rubbed his chest, and whispered, "You like that?"

Gregory could only say, "Uh-huh."

She replied, "Drive me home or help me get a cab home. We can talk more about that when we can get together again."

They left the lounge holding hands and talking, and several of Gregory's colleagues waved and smiled as they exited the lounge. Outside, the smell of barbeque was in the air; a warm, gentle summer breeze moved across their bodies and faces; and they kissed fervently in the light of a full moon and a street full of people. After those moments, they decided to get food and take it to his place to eat.

As they drove to his place, they gently rubbed on one another's leg, and Gregory felt that this was one of those inimitable moments in life that had to be consummated with more than just a quick fuck. So, when he had parked the car in the garage of his condo, he left the car running, the door open, and the music on. Stella did not attempt to get out of the car until he had opened her door, taken her hand, and helped her out of the car, leaving that door open, too. She smiled when he pulled her into his arms and started to slow dance with her in the garage to a tune by the Whispers called "Are You Going My Way."

Tears of joy rolled down Stella's face, and she said: "I got it."

As soon as they got in the door of his condo, they opened the food, got glasses of champagne to drink, and settled on his couch with the Whispers singing some of their top hits. They never got far into that part of the evening. They only had a few bites of the barbeque ribs and shrimp and a few sips of champagne before he took her hand and led her into his bedroom.

After a few hours of exquisite lovemaking, she whispered in his ear a few words from the Whispers' tune they had danced to in the garage: "Make me your future or lock me in your history."

He cried softly as he held her gently and whispered in her ear: "I want to make you my future."

Exhausted by their lovemaking and exhilarated by the intimacy of the evening, they fell asleep holding one another and smiling.

They had made love and fallen asleep with the blinds of the bedroom open. He had a panoramic view of the city that always enhanced his lovemaking activities in his condo. At the break of dawn, the sun offered a warm glow off of the lake and a spectacular view of the city whose buildings' lights were still on from the previous night.

She woke up first; but when she shifted in his bed, he quietly told her to stay there and he would bring her breakfast in bed. Stella smiled and said, "I assume you do this for all of your ladies, but I am going to act like I am special and that you are only doing this for me."

Gregory replied, "That's a good way to act, and it's my first way of showing you that I want to make you my future. Here's the remote so you can watch whatever you like on TV while I make breakfast for us. Cream and sugar in your coffee?"

Stella smiled and said, "Yes. And you back in the bed when we have finished eating!"

After eating breakfast and then making love, they slept for a few hours. They woke up to the sound of her beeper going off. He said to her, "This is Saturday. You still have to work?"

She grimaced and replied, "Oh. I forgot to tell you that I work for the Chicago Police Department. I am a captain in the detective division, so I am on call 24/7. Sorry, we did not get into more conversation about our lives before we moved into this phase of our relationship. You ok?"

He stared into her oval, beautiful face and said, "I am good. Call me when you take care of whatever you have to do. Now that I know what you do, I am sure I will worry about you."

She became a little teary-eyed and said: "I've done this for a while now, and I know a little about taking care of myself in the streets. But I will be a little more cautious so that I can get back to you and in your bed."

She smiled, got up, washed up, dressed, blew him a kiss, headed for the door, and said, "Make plans for us for the evening. I will call you shortly. I will take a cab to the police station, which is only a few blocks from here. Bye."

After Stella left his place, Gregory shuddered a bit after thinking about what he had gotten himself into. He also grinned when he thought about the past evening and the recent morning that delighted him in so many ways.

Stella was an aggressive woman, which was partly explained by the line of work she was in. She was also a gentle soul, as revealed by her subtle lovemaking and conversation. What he liked and loved most about Stella was that she appeared to be one of the most authentic people he had ever known.

That sense of authenticity he got from Stella left him a little uneasy and in a quandary. Oddly enough, that feeling and state of mind also made him even more attracted to Stella. Somehow thinking about Stella made him think about taking her to Lawry's, a steak house, for dinner that evening.

He smiled at that notion of associating Stella with the idea of a carnivore, but then he tried to think about what else they might do, beyond the obvious, later in the day. He could only come up with a set at the Jazz Showcase featuring McCoy Tyner's ensemble.

At this point in his life, McCoy Tyner was his all-time favorite musician, after Charlie Parker, of course. So, he was happy to see him perform in person at the Jazz Showcase, then located on Rush Street. He also recognized that Lawry's was not far from the Jazz Showcase, so this was not only going to be a fun evening (for many reasons) but also one easy to navigate.

As he cleaned up his condo while he waited to hear from Stella, he smiled and thought about one of his favorite writers, Walter Mosley. He had read almost every book written by Mosley, but he was never sure what he liked most about his books. For sure, he liked the fearlessness of most of the characters in his novels, especially the protagonists like Easy Rawlins from one of his first novels, "Devil in A Blue Dress."

He also liked Mosley's facility with the English language, not just in terms of words used, but the way he could "turn a phrase," as the old folks used to say. What he liked most about Mosley, however, is the way he allowed his characters to be in the world almost without judgment of any kind, especially those judgments based primarily upon Judeo-Christian values.

Gregory had grown up in a non-denominational church called Unity, which tried to adhere to some of the teachings of Christianity without all of the canonical trappings of some other religious denominations.

And while he had on his own developed a moral center based upon just what made sense to him, he understood that a lot of his moral center came from what he had learned over the years as a child and young man at that storefront church on 43rd and Michigan on the South Side of Chicago.

So, as he read the books of Walter Mosley and marveled at the characters' willingness to bend the truth and often skirt physical harm or death of themselves or others by engaging in transgressions most people would not even entertain, he recognized that those characters were all of us under the right conditions or circumstances.

That thought helped him be a lot more comfortable with Stella out there in the streets because he understood that she would sometimes be faced with life and death decisions or choices that could only be right or wrong or good or bad if viewed from within a particular system of beliefs. He smiled at that bit of existential and transcendental thought.

Stella called him that afternoon to tell him that she might be a little late for their night out together because she had just been assigned to a murder case: a black woman who had been found dead in an alley on the southeast side; she had been shot execution-style—in the back of the head.

She called him at 7:00 to tell him to meet her at Lawry's at 7:30. He told her he would do that and then said: "Kisses all over."

She replied, "Is that a tease or a promise."

He said, "Both."

Chapter Fifteen
Life in the City

He took a cab to Lawry's because he knew that Stella would be driving, and having two cars would just complicate the transportation part of the evening. Besides, he liked the idea of being chauffeured around by a lady, which meant both of his hands would be free to engage in a bit of mischief.

When he entered Lawry's, the hostess greeted him, nodded her head in a particular direction, and said: "She's waiting for you over this way, sir. Follow me."

As soon as he sat, he said, "How did she know to direct me to you."

Stella replied, "I told her I was expecting a gentleman who was handsome, well dressed, and distinguished looking. I also told her just to bring the first gentleman who met those criteria to me."

They both smiled and then laughed at that bit of humor from Stella.

He started to sit across from Stella at the curved table but decided that would put him too far away from her. So, he went and sat next to her in a chair that was on her right. He smiled at that move because he knew that position would allow her to view his best profile. He then leaned over and kissed her lightly on the lips and said, "How are you darling?"

She smiled and said, "I am good, baby. How are you?"

At that moment, the waiter approached with menus and a wine list. He asked: "Have you dined with us before?"

Stella replied, "He has, but I have not had the pleasure of dining here."

The waiter replied, "The gentleman knows the quality of the dining experience here, and I will make sure your experience here meets or exceeds that of the gentleman's. Can I start the evening by getting drinks for you?"

Stella looked in the direction of the waiter and said, "A bottle of Moet, please."

As soon as the waiter left, she then looked at Gregory, smiled, and said: "Are you comfortable with me taking charge here."

Gregory smiled and said, "Yes. I am okay with you taking the lead in this situation. That is what you do, isn't it? And I will still pay for dinner or split it with you or let you pay for it all."

She stared into his eyes and said, "You are confident and self-assured, aren't you?"

He replied, "Yes. And I like confident and self-assured women. Then he leaned in and kissed her lips with a little more fervor than before. She smiled at that move, and she took his hand and held it in both of her hands for a moment before saying: "I could get used to this."

For dinner, they decided on lobster bisque soup, a shared Caesar salad with shaved parmesan cheese, and medium-well rib-eye steaks. After they had champagne in hand, they toasted to "life and love!"

They continued to hold hands, smile at each other, sip the cold champagne, and coo until the soup arrived. They agreed that the soup was an excellent start to what the waiter had promised would be a good dining experience.

When they had finished eating, the waiter brought the dessert menus and asked, "How was the meal?"

Stella looked the waiter in the eyes. She then said almost sensuously, "It exceeded my expectations. Thank you for a great dining experience."

The waiter said, "Great! Thank you, madam! I will share that with the chef and the kitchen. Your dessert is on me, and I will also throw in another bottle of champagne. Free!"

After they had finished the dessert and champagne, they just sat and looked at one another without talking verbally. However, they were still communicating by just looking at each other and smiling, her eyes reflecting some light from a source that was behind him. She said at some point, "What's on the agenda for the rest of the evening?"

He smiled and enthusiastically blurted out: "McCoy Tyner and me."

She guffawed and grabbed his hand and said: "Always ready with a plan for a good time. I like hanging with you! I got dinner, and I don't want a discussion about it."

He just stared at her with a coy smile, but he was thinking: *Quite the woman*!

They stood outside of the restaurant and held hands as they waited for her silver BMW to be brought from the parking lot by the valet. Neither seemed inclined to want to talk much as they stood there enjoying the warmth of the evening and the laughter of people headed to some unknown destinations. She pulled him closer to her, slipped her arm around his waist, and kissed him ever so lightly.

She then said, "The woman who was shot that I told you about earlier was my half-sister that I had not seen for a while. At one point, we ran the streets together for a long time, and then she met a dude that was good to her in many ways, but he somehow was associated with Chicago's underworld. I told you that it was probably not a robbery because she had all of her valuables on her."

He said, "So how are you feeling now? Are you sure you want to be out now?"

She said, "I am fine, and I am going to get the motherfucker who killed her!"

Gregory turned her so that he could fully embrace her face-to-face to see if he could give her solace of some kind. With that gesture, she laid her cheek on his shoulder and quietly sobbed. He knew he had given her all that he could at that moment, so he offered to drive them to the Jazz Showcase to provide her with a little more time to grieve without having to pay attention to anything else.

There was a huge crowd that showed up to see McCoy Tyner that evening. Even at that, they were ushered into a reserved section of the place. Gregory always chose the reserved section of the Jazz Showcase even though it was twice as expensive as the seating in other areas of the venue. He had gotten to know the owner and his son over the years because of his frequent visits to the club and the fact that he always got reserved seats unless they were not available.

Tyner started his first set with a few pieces from his recently released album, *Inner Voices*, which featured various musicians on different cuts on the album. The band started the evening with a tune called "For Tomorrow," a piece that has a chorus singing behind the band on the album but not for this live set.

Always looking serious when he plays; that evening, Tyner wowed the crowd with a variety of pieces from his various albums put out over the years. He had seen Tyner in various settings, and he always enjoyed the intensity of his playing, even of pieces that had a slow tempo.

On one of the slower numbers by Tyner, out of the corner of his left eye, he could see tears streaming down Stella's face. He placed his left hand around her shoulder and pulled her closer to him.

He said, "Would you like to leave?"

She shook her head and whispered, "No."

They did sit through the one set, and he decided to take her home with him so that she would not be alone. She told him she wanted to be at her place and he could come and be with her there. This time she asked that he drive, although he had no idea of where she lived. As they drove away from the Jazz Showcase, she told him that she lived in an area of Chicago called River North, and she gave him directions for getting there.

As they sat in her high-rise apartment on the 22nd floor of a building on Superior and Wells not too far from the jazz place, she asked if he would get them both a glass of champagne while she tried to take herself to a place of less heartbreak. She pointed to a cabinet with champagne glasses and told him the champagne was on a door shelf inside the refrigerator.

Looking out at the city's view of the downtown area, Stella said, "I just need to talk a bit. Do you mind if I unload a bit?"

He said, "No. I find it is always helpful to share a burden with others. It lightens the load that has to be carried."

She began by saying, "I have thought a lot about what happened to my sister and why. There are all sorts of possible scenarios surrounding her death. One scenario has to do with the dude she was involved with who is connected to the criminal element here in Chicago. Another has to do with her ex-husband, who had taken out an insurance policy on her for a million dollars before they were divorced. Then there is the situation where she testified against a gang member who committed sodomy with a young boy some years earlier. He had gotten ten years for that."

Gregory stared hard at Stella and thought to himself, *What the fuck have I gotten myself into?*

He finally said, "Are you sure you want to handle this case? Won't it be hard on you to have a constant reminder of your sister's death and how she died?"

Stella replied: "No, not handling this case would be hard on me. I would still think about her and feel that not enough was being done to solve the case. So, I am going to be better off being out there looking for the person who killed her."

Stella moved closer to Gregory and laid her head in his chest and sobbed for a few minutes as he stared at the north view of the city with its unbelievable buildings and seductive lights.

He said: "I understand, and I agree with that assessment."

And with those few words, he took her to her bed and held her tightly as they lapsed into a deep sleep that brought them into the next day. They were again awakened by the sound of her beeper, and she shook him to tell him again that duty called and that she had to go.

After Stella waved goodbye and left her apartment, he turned on his left side, picked up his cellphone, and called Sharon, his ex-wife that he had not spoken to or seen for several months. When he decided to call Sharon, he wasn't exactly sure how she might help Stella with her sister's murder. He did know that Sharon's ex-husband was a cop and Sharon's friend was married to a captain in the police department. There was no answer.

He scribbled a note for Stella telling her that he was taking a cab home to get started on some research related to his pursuit of his

PhD. He also told her that he was trying to think of ways he could help her solve the case associated with the murder of her sister. He did not tell her that he was trying to get individuals he indirectly knew to get involved in the case or that the research that he was doing was also related to her sister's death.

After he arrived home, he got a gin and tonic drink and sat in a designer chair (that can now be seen at the Art Institute of Chicago) in a room off of his kitchen and tried to see what he could think of as a starting point for research related to Stella's sister. Since he had not been able to reach anyone he directly or indirectly knew who was connected to the Chicago Police Department, he picked up his house phone and dialed the number of a buddy who worked for the Cook County Sheriff's Department.

His buddy from the sheriff's department was able to tell him that word on the street was that the murder was probably a "revenge killing" and that it was probably done by a single individual. He continued to sit in the room off of the kitchen and sip his gin and tonic.

With that bit of information from his buddy in the sheriff's department, he went over the scenarios Stella had offered regarding her sister's death. Almost all of the scenarios pointed to someone who might have well committed the crime.

Chapter Sixteen
And It All Goes Round and Round

Gregory continued to sit in the room off the kitchen and now sipped a third gin and tonic and think about the scenarios Stella had told him about related to her sister's murder. He thought about the petty criminal Stella's sister had recently dated, and he decided to start there. He made a call to Sharon to ask if her close friend (whose place he had first been able to socialize with Sharon) would ask her husband (a captain in the Chicago Police Department) to gather information about the friend of Stella's sister.

A day later, Gregory got a call from Sharon saying that the police captain had told her that the petty criminal had been in the lockup a few days before and after the murder so he could eliminate that scenario as a relevant one to continue to pursue. Gregory thought to himself, *one down, three to go.*

When he told Stella about what he had been able to find out, she thanked him and said, "I don't know that we can forget about him as a suspect or at least someone connected to her murder. He might have been able to have someone he knows commit the murder, knowing that he would have a perfect alibi. But let's talk about scenario number two."

Stella started the discussion of scenario number two by saying, "Out of all the scenarios I have talked to you about, the one I like most is the one related to her ex-husband who took out a million-dollar insurance policy on my sister before they were divorced. I like that because it easily follows the old triad for solving crimes or mysteries: means, motive, and opportunity."

Gregory smiled and said, "Uh-huh."

Stella then said, "The only problem with that scenario is the clause in the policy that says the insurance can't be collected if the person who is insured is either killed by caused to be killed by the beneficiary of the insurance policy. So that may be an issue, at least for the time being, for the ex-husband. But that said, he is still very much a suspect in the murder of my sister."

Gregory said, "tell me a little about your sister."

Moisture appeared around Stella's eyes before she spoke, but she finally said: "Well, in some ways, she was a real bitch. In other ways, she was a genuinely kind soul. I always had a hard time reconciling those two dimensions of my sister, but it may not matter now."

Stella just sat and stared out of the windows of his apartment for several minutes before she spoke again. Then she said, "You would have liked my sister. She wasn't well educated, but she had a sharp mind. She also enjoyed running the streets and jumping in out of the bed of various people, including a few women that she had known over the years. She never wanted to get married, but she always talked about having a few kids to help her feel that she had had a complete and well-rounded life.

"I never liked what she was about as a person, mostly because I felt she would never achieve her full potential or be close to being an authentic person, whatever that means. However, I loved her and, in some ways, was envious of the way she lived her life. That I wanted more for her than she seemed to want for herself never really made sense to me, but that is what I have always desired."

Stella stopped talking at that point and just grabbed Gregory's hand and started walking to the door. Gregory decided to just be in the flow and did not inquire about where they were headed. When they were outside of his place looking north at the gorgeous and wonderous Chicago downtown skyline, Stella gently pulled Gregory's hand to guide him north on Clark Street.

It was one of those matchless summer evenings in late July when the city was bathed in warm breezes off the lake and gusts of warm air from the Gulf of Mexico. Gregory smiled but still said nothing as they walked north on Clark Street. When they were close to Polk Street, Stella said, "Let's have dinner outside at Sociale. I hear they have added some items to their menu that now includes Crab cakes and a few other items I think you would enjoy."

Gregory responded with a simple, "Okay."

As they sat outside of the restaurant and watched cars and people constantly going north and south and east and west, neither of them seemed inclined to talk at first until Stella said, "You know I love you?"

Gregory simply nodded his head to signify a yes.

Stella said, "So this is what I want from you tonight and in the near future. This evening I want you to buy me dinner and an expensive bottle of champagne. It does not have to be too expensive. Moet is fine. Then I want you to take me around the corner to the Jazz Showcase to see one of our favorite vocalists, Dee Alexander, and her ensemble. There I want you to buy me another bottle or two of expensive champagne and hold me tight for the whole evening.

Gregory said, "Is that it?"

Stella said, "That's it in terms of the evening. For the near future, I want us to live together and have a child or two. We don't even have to be married unless that is something we both want and or need. We can buy a condo here in the city or move to a house in the suburb. I am open to either one, although I am inclined to stay in the city. Staying in the city is partly because I can hang on to the memory of my sister."

Gregory said, "What about your desire to catch your sister's killer."

Stella replied, "I will still work on her case as long as they allow me to. But as we stood in your place and talked about her death and what I had always wanted for her in terms of a life, I realized that whatever I did or did not do from this point on would never bring her back or allow her to have the life I wanted for her. At that moment, I flashed back to us dancing in the garage and the question I posed to you and the answer you gave me. So, now I want you to make me your future, and I want to make you mine."

Gregory smiled, took Stella's hands, and leaned over to gently kiss her. As he did so, he heard a song playing on the restaurant's outside speakers. It was a tune he knew well but hadn't heard in more than a decade, despite him having it in his collection. It was a tune featuring Irene Kral singing and Junior Mance on piano: "This Is Always."

Epilogue

This isn't sometimes, this is always
This isn't maybe, this is always
This is love, the real beginning of forever

This isn't just midsummer madness
A passing glow, a moment's gladness
Yes it's love, I knew it on the night we met

You tied a string around my heart
So how can I forget you?

From the song, "This Is Always"—Lyrics by Mack Gordon

Printed in the United States
by Baker & Taylor Publisher Services